# THE SHIP WE BUILT

by Lexie Bean

illustrated by Noah Grigni

DIAL BOOKS

Dial Books
An imprint of Penguin Random House LLC, New York

Text copyright © 2020 by Lexie Bean
Illustrations copyright © 2020 by Noah Grigni

The author will be donating a portion of their royalties to ACTOUT, class and
community space for LGBTQIA+ artists.

Visit us online at penguinrandomhouse.com

Library of Congress Cataloging-in-Publication Data
Names: Bean, Lexie, author. | Grigni, Noah, illustrator. Title: The ship we built / by Lexie Bean;
illustrated by Noah Grigni. Description: New York : Dial Books, [2020] | Audience: Ages 10–14. |
Audience: Grades 7–9. | Summary: A fifth grader whose best friends walked away, whose mother is
detached, and whose father does unspeakable things, copes with the help of their friend Sofie and
anonymous letters tied to balloons and released. Includes a list of resources related to abuse, gender,
sexuality, and more. Identifiers: LCCN 2019051654 (print) | LCCN 2019051655 (ebook) |
ISBN 9780525554837 (hardcover) | ISBN 9780525554844 (ebook)
Subjects: CYAC: Gender identity—Fiction. | Letters—Fiction. | Middle schools—Fiction. | Schools—
Fiction. | Family life—Fiction. | Sexual abuse—Fiction. | Best friends—Fiction. | Friendship—Fiction.
Classification: LCC PZ7.1.B427 Shi 2020 (print) | LCC PZ7.1.B427 (ebook) | DDC [Fic]—dc23

Printed in the United States of America
1 3 5 7 9 10 8 6 4 2

Design by Mina Chung
Text set in Albertina MT

*For all the boys who didn't know who they could grow up to be;*
*for ten-year-old me*

Dear Whoever Gets This Letter,

I used to hum happy songs on my way to school. Today I just kept my mouth straight and made up excuses to stop and pretend to tie my shoes. It was the first day of the fifth grade, which I heard is never easy. When I finally reached the flag-pole outside of William Henderson Elementary, I kneeled down by the dewy grass to tighten my already double-knotted laces. I wanted to make myself small and easy for groups of friends to step over me. Their backpacks were mostly empty and the girls didn't look back once.

In case you find this letter, you should know that our school is in the Upper Peninsula, not in the downstate part of Michigan that's shaped like a hand. Some people here say we're in God's Country because it's so beautiful, but the truth is that a lot of mapmakers forget to even include us on their maps because so much of the land is just forest and abandoned mines. My mom always jokes, "We're actu-ally everything that The Hand let go of," but she never laughs when she says it. I think that's her way of saying that some-times life can get hard because God gets busy in other places or reads the wrong maps. Maybe she's right, or maybe the people who say we live in "God's Country" are right. I am not so sure sometimes. I guess you should also know that everyone calls me Ellie. It has never been my favorite, but I guess you can call me that too.

Anyway, the first day of school can be a tough one because over the summertime friends miss a lot of each other changing. Some of us get taller or different haircuts and some of us get new trampolines. Some of us move houses or get more secrets.

This first day was extra tough because a lot of my friends have decided that I am too weird. They say it is weird that I sometimes call myself a boy, and they don't like me now for some other reasons too. These friends are all girls, but we actually like a lot of the same things. We like seeing dogs on the street, Hula-Hooping, ice-skating, watching *Boy Meets World*, and eating pepperoni pizza. Do you like those things? It's okay if you like other stuff too. To be honest, I don't really care if the person reading this is a boy or a girl, but for some reason picking sides seems to matter more now than ever.

Hope your day was better than mine.

Sincerely,
Ellie Beck

Dear Whoever You Are,

I hope that you find this letter, and that you'll read it and won't throw it away. I have some things to tell you. I hope that's okay. I've been just feeling kind of alone.

This summer, all of my BFFs—Courtney, Gina, and Mary—just wanted to read magazines that have quizzes for fun, horoscopes, and things that the stars say. They didn't even want to go berry picking like we used to. Instead we had makeovers, and they called me "the most improved" when they gave me eyeliner. A few of them even used yellow highlighters from their back-to-school shopping to make their hair more blond-looking. You'd think they would have known highlighters are for books, because they all have professor parents that teach at that big university across town. The point is that these friends started a new club at the end of summer vacation without me.

It happened when Courtney had a big slumber party, and almost everybody got under the backyard trampoline that was the size of a swimming pool. They huddled together, and pointed at me from under the shade until it was obvious

I was un-invited. You would have thought I had mad cow disease. The thing is, I don't.

I have to admit, I got the idea to write this letter while I was at that slumber party. Courtney had a lot of balloons that stood so confidently around the table full of presents, but there was one pink balloon that got away. I bet I was the only person in the backyard to notice since they were all too busy laughing over that "I'm a Barbie girl in a Barbie world" song. The balloon floated up and up until it was too far to see. Watching it disappear gave me a bright idea. If I attached a letter to a balloon, and secretly let it free from my bedroom window, it could be a way to meet someone new. At the very least, I could meet someone who wasn't at that dang party.

I stood there alone on the deck with the party balloons for so long. I felt my arms and ears getting burned by the sun. All the confetti cake was gone and the chip bowl was empty with only yellow crumbs on the bottom. Courtney's unwrapped presents sat lonely on the table. I tell you what, her new pink hunting jacket, the T-shirt that said boy crazy, and bottle of cucumber melon lotion all just stared at me. There was nothing in that backyard for me. The song on the boom box changed, but the girls kept laughing and pointing. Even that stupid bobblehead owl perched on the fence gave me a funny look.

I finally went inside through the noisy screen door. Courtney's big sister was watching me too. I don't think she likes me so much either. She's a high schooler and wears purple spray to smell like a celebrity. She stuck to her side of the room, and turned up the volume on her music video countdown show when I picked up their house phone to call my mom.

All Mom said was "Ready yet?" She said it loud over Dad's TV in the background. I nodded my head as if she could hear me.

I tried my best not to look at Courtney's big sister when I hung up the plastic phone. I swear she didn't move an inch the whole time. I rolled up my sleeping bag and looked for my socks super fast, trying not to block her view of Tim McGraw singing in a palace. I put on my backpack and left behind the goodie bag with a pencil and scoubidou keychain on purpose.

On the front steps, I sat down next to an ant castle and watched the little bugs build their home with rocks. I don't know how they carry things that seem so much bigger than them. The concrete felt cold on my legs, and Mom was taking forever to come pick me up. Five red pickup trucks, two white ones, and so many teenagers on bikes passed by, but not my mom's noisy blue car with that peeling "906" area code bumper sticker. I bet Mom was busy buying radio bingo cards or putting pop cans in that grocery store machine. Or maybe she got busy watching TV with Dad. I don't know.

I have to admit, though, after about twenty minutes of alone time, one person joined me on the front porch. Her name is Sofie Gavia. She sat only a few inches away and watched the street with me. I hoped right away that none of the girls from the backyard could see us together like that. I'm surprised she left the trampoline at all, but I guess she was mostly quiet at the birthday party too. I think she was only invited because some of the moms are PTO friends, which is just a secret club for parents to talk about school in their free time for some reason.

I didn't really want to talk to Sofie even though she's really, really nice. I just wanted to be alone and keep quiet, but I didn't want to be alone either. It's kind of hard to explain. I tried turning my knees away from Sofie so she would get the hint, but she broke the silence anyways.

She turned her head and said "I like your shoes" like she meant it. You should know that my shoes aren't anything special. They're just white with green laces. I tried ignoring her, but then she said, "Do you want some of my lemonade?" and she held her red cup closer to me. Don't judge me, but I decided to reach for it. When I turned around, I noticed that Sofie and I actually had matching scraped knees. You didn't hear any of this from me, though. Word gets around fast and pretty much everyone who was at that dang slumber party is also in Mr. B's class with me this year.

Yesterday, on our first day of school, I was just hoping to hide behind my notebooks all day long, make things easier for everybody. But that didn't work for me at all. Instead, Mr. B gave us our first big lesson. He tried to teach us the important lesson of walking into a room with more confidence. Courtney's big sister had warned us about this if we got Mr. B for the fifth grade, but it sounded way less scary back when I had my friends. How am I supposed to walk into a room with confidence if nobody wants me there? Do you know what I mean?

It was bad. We all had to stand as straight as we could along the white brick wall, taking turns leaving and coming back to the classroom with our hands on our hips. Mr. B shouted, "EXPAND!" and wrote it in all capital letters in the top corner of the chalkboard that never gets washed away. He then said, "You can become bigger than this room." How the heck am I supposed to "EXPAND!" when everyone cool now uses bubble-letters and makes themselves into small groups under backyard trampolines? A lot of the other kids in my class crossed their arms and looked nervous to try their walks, but I still think that they all had better walks than I did.

I'm starting to think that people only were ever nice to me because I used to be the new kid at school from White Pine. When I was brand-new, everybody wanted to say hi when I walked into the room. Now I'm just regular, or maybe even less than regular. I could tell Sofie had a hard time with her walk too. We both had to do it three or four times until we could look up from the floor. I hope nobody noticed that she and I have that in common. If people didn't already think that I'm weird, they are for sure going to think that now, right? Actually, please don't answer that. I don't want to know.

I will say that Dylan Beaman walked so confidently in the first round. He moved slow and steady in his Red Wings jersey. His posture was all the way straight and his shoes lit up too. I wish you could have seen it. My old friends sure did talk about him a lot, so I feel pretty lucky that Dylan and my last names are close to each other in the alphabet and so our assigned seats are right next to each other. It made it a little easier not to hide behind my notebook all day long or anything like that.

When Dylan Beaman got to his desk today, he pulled out his folder that has a lightning bolt on it and said "Hi." He really did say hi to me. I thought about telling him that I like storms too. Instead, I fixed my headband and made sure all my freshly sharpened pencils were lined up perfectly in rainbow order. I just hope I didn't totally blow my chance of getting another "Hi" from Dylan Beaman this week. Maybe one day, my confident walk will be as good as his. That way, Dylan will see it and realize that maybe we have a lot in common, even though my paper folders are just plain-colored and my shoes don't light up.

When did the word *hi* get so hard. Why did walking get so hard? Maybe there is something wrong with me after all. I just wish Courtney didn't always fold her arms when she looks at me now. We didn't even say hi to each other, and we have already had two whole entire days of school. We haven't spoken ever since I blew it at her stupid slumber party. I wonder if I will be invited to one ever again.

If you still have your friends, maybe you can give me some ideas on how to get mine back. Even though we're now in fifth grade, my old BFFs look pretty enough to be in middle school. All three of them crimped their hair like cowgirls for the first week of school. I didn't even think to do that. I'm starting to think that I should pretend my parents went to college or moved to Houghton from somewhere fancy, like Milwaukee or Lansing. Maybe I should pretend to be a girl again. I don't know. For now, I guess it's good that all our last names are so different and so all of those girls sit in different parts of the classroom.

It's also good that Mr. B has so many inspiration posters in his class, because I have somewhere to put my eyes when I feel anybody looking at me now. One of the posters says *Do your personal best*, and another one has a big rainbow on it. My favorite poster has a big picture of cheese, but I can't exactly remember what it says. Sofie's seat is actually right under that one. I wasn't going to tell you this, but she turned around and waved to me just as our very first class was starting. Nobody else saw it, I think. I just looked down at my *Little Mermaid* Band-Aid and wondered if Sofie's knees had already healed.

If I could make my own inspiration poster, it would say *It's* more fun on top of the trampoline anyways because that's where you can jump, pretend you're an astronaut, or have a flat place to draw all the things you can see from real high up. I'll draw a picture of my poster in this letter for you. That way, you can hang it up where you need inspiration or maybe just use the paper to make a hat if you hate your haircut. Mine's growing funny too. I didn't get a haircut this summer, but I did get more secrets. I can't tell them to you right now, but maybe some-day soon.

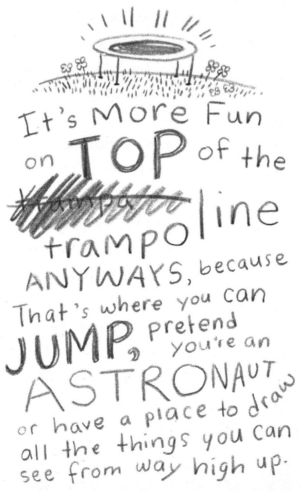

If you find this balloon letter, please leave your response buried under the WELCOME TO HOUGHTON: BIRTHPLACE OF NATIONAL HOCKEY sign next to Portage Bridge. You can't miss it. I'll check there tomorrow or the next day. I love getting mail, even though it hardly ever happens.

Sincerely,
Ellie Beck

Tuesday, September 9, 1997

Hi again,

Good news, I found a quarter on the floor in the cafeteria today. I put it in my pocket right away and used it to buy a balloon at that blue gas station kitty-corner from the Family Videos. The cashier's name is Björn. He asked me, "Is it your birthday?" It's not, but I do think balloons are a nice way to celebrate something even if nobody else does. There's hardly anyone ever in that store, so I bet he was just trying to make some nice conversation. Anyways, I hope you get this letter just when you needed someone to say hi to you too.

I hate to ask this, but are you thinking about people you miss? I am all the time.

My friends and I all used to draw together at lunchtime. We would make flowers and clouds, and Gina even showed us how to do cool-shaped *S*'s and even 3-D boxes. I spent most of my time at lunch today drawing on my yellow foam tray alone. I mentioned in my last letter that I would share a secret, so here it goes. It's a really good drawing secret. My go-to doodles are jellyfish and wheels of Swiss cheese. They might seem really different from each other, but in drawing them they actually look exactly the same. The only real difference is that one of them has arms that reach down into the water. The other one just stays a circle.

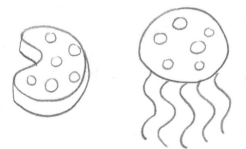

The cafeteria is not a good place for secrets because it's one of the biggest rooms at school. It's also the same place we have gym class and Jump Rope for Heart assemblies, and every word echoes off the walls. The tables are long and brown, and somehow feel lonely even when we are all squished together side by side. Is there anyone you can tell all your secrets to? My old friends and I used to tell them to each other at recess. I'm really starting to wish I didn't tell them my secret about being a boy. Maybe some things should just stay secret.

Back when things were okay, Courtney, Gina, Mary, and I would sit by this big maple tree in the little woods behind school. We called it our Secrets Tree. Sometimes we would pull petals off of nearby daisies to ask, "He loves me? He loves me not?" I'm not sure any of us knew who "He" was. But now, the girls kick boys' legs under the tables. Their feet sometimes bounce the surface, which makes it hard to have a steady hand for drawing. I bet people don't ask daisies for love advice anymore.

The fifth grade isn't like other years. We used to have burping contests with boys and girls together. Now burping contests are boys-only and my old friends have squeaky new laughs. The girls laugh extra hard when Dylan Beaman pops his potato chip bag super-duper loud. He presses into the yellow plastic with all his strength until the air jumps out real fast and makes a sound as like thunder. He always bites his lip and smiles afterward, like he knows he can do big things in this world. Do you ever accidentally laugh when you don't really mean it? I hate to say it, but sometimes I giggle with everyone at Dylan Beaman's pop-sound too, even when it hurts my ears more than my plastic headband.

But today was special. Dylan Beaman opened his potato

chip bag like a normal person, and then he actually shared some of the insides with me. That was nice, because I didn't have anything good in my lunch to trade with him, like one of those juices in the shiny pouches or a Ring Pop. I took the tiniest chip, but it still tasted delicious. To top it all off, he then said, "You can join in on the burping contest if you want to." Can you believe it? He for sure knows that it's only boys now. For a second, it felt like he really got me.

Of course, all my old friends turned their heads when I followed Dylan to the other side of the long table. I couldn't hear what they were gossiping about, but I didn't even care. I kept my eyes on Dylan's American flag shirt and noticed that he got the tiniest haircut last night. The shaved sides were smoother than ever when he looked behind his shoulder to make sure I was still there. He smiled, at least I think he did. Maybe he remembered from last year that I'm pretty good at burping after eating apples and taking sips of chocolate milk. I actually got third place for the whole entire fourth grade.

As soon as we sat down, I remembered again that those days are over. It was real obvious that I'm not like the other boys in class. Their voices are much bigger. They like to wear green camouflage and hide their moms' catalogs under their beds. They stomp their feet and shout each other's names like they really mean it at every burping contest. They never did that back when girls were allowed to burp too.

I looked over to my old friends to see if it was also obvious to them that I didn't belong there, but they had already forgotten about me. They were all leaning over their brand-new cootie catcher, pointing at the different folds. What's worse—when I looked back to Dylan and the rest of the boys-only burping contest, they had already skipped over me, cheering on somebody I don't even know.

When Dylan Beaman said I could join, I didn't realize that it was only to watch from the sidelines. I don't think any of them cared about how good I could be. The whole time I just smiled halfway and played with my hangnail until it bled. Two of the boys leaned over me and gave each other high fives like they forgot I was in the middle. I thought my carton of milk was going to fall over. I betcha I would have had success if I had one of those fancy pizza Lunchables or if I joined the homeroom basketball team and spun a ball on just one of my fingers like Michael Jordan. Maybe that way, the boys would have let me play or decide to invite me more than just this one time.

Maybe it's a good thing Dylan Beaman wanted me there watching. At the last slumber party with my old friends, almost every girl screamed when Courtney shared her dream of riding bikes and eating fudge with Dylan on Mackinac Island. We then had to practice saying our names with his last name over and over again. I would be called Ellie Beaman. I kind of like how it sounds, but I could never think about doodling that name since our desks are right next to each other. I hope you are good at keeping secrets, because I wouldn't say this to just anybody. I hope I eventually have good things in my lunch to trade with Dylan Beaman. That way, he would be happy to see me and we can try the burping contest again. That's even more than just saying hi. I don't know.

I've considered taking my lunch to the bathroom stall just to make lunch easier, but I'm worried that's never going to happen as long as the lunch aids are in charge of us. The aid in the doorway wears pants just like my mom, the kind that make those loud swish-swish sounds whenever she walks. The lunch aid also has a red plastic whistle around her neck for when we get too loud or when it seems like someone is going to get into big trouble. If I tried to leave, she would blow that whistle super-duper loud. I don't want everyone and their brother looking at me just because I want to do something different. Don't you know that having a little privacy is why I would want to go to the bathroom stall to begin with?

What would you do if you were me? It has only been like seven days of school, and I still don't really know where to put myself. Maybe nowhere is the right place to sit. Do you ever feel like you made up the good times? Does that happen to everybody? With any luck, maybe I will find someone to draw on the lunch trays with me. If you happen to find this balloon, please write me back soon. I have been checking for letters under the WELCOME TO HOUGHTON sign nearly every day after school. Maybe you and I will draw together or share chocolate milk there one day? I don't know, maybe if you wanted to.

Sincerely,
Ellie

P.S. What do you think of the name Sawyer? I think it's nice.

Monday, September 14, 1997

Hello Friend,

Guess what? I have the best news. Even though I have over-heard Dad say a million times that "money is tight," he says I'm now old enough to get a one-dollar allowance. This means I can afford a chocolate milk and also a balloon to write more letters every week. All I have to do is make my bed and wash my own dishes every day, which is super easy.

Do you know what else is good news? Dylan shared another potato chip with me at lunch the other day. He didn't invite me to the boys-only burping contest after that, but it was still a really nice thing to do. Also, it turns out all I had to do was ask, "May I go to the bathroom, please?" and the lunch aid lady totally lets me. What she doesn't know is that I sometimes stay in the stall until the bell rings. It's not perfect, but it's better than sitting at those lunch tables with everybody else. It gets too lonely to watch all the other fifth graders talking and trading their lunches with each other. I tried playing the "He loves me? He loves me not?" game using a string cheese, but instead of "He," I was just thinking about my old friends.

Actually, Courtney did talk to me earlier this week, but it didn't last long. It was only because Mr. B assigned me the Language Arts binder with a number thirty-two on the spine. Everybody wanted to trade with me because thirty-two is also the TV channel for MTV. Courtney got all mad when I shook my head. She said in front of everybody, "It's not like you watch MTV anyways."

I hate to say it, but Courtney was right. I only said no to trading because I thought maybe she would ask me again or maybe she would just think I am cool for having it. No such luck. Instead, everybody went to talk to the quiet boy in class who got the VH1 binder. Now I just bring my MTV binder with me everywhere I go just in case anyone maybe wants to talk to me about it again. I open it up as wide as I can at recess and when I'm waiting at my desk for class to start. I even hold my binder tight between my legs when standing at the bathroom sinks. It's hard to keep it from falling onto the tile floor, especially when my old friends are there. They wash their hands much faster than I do.

I like being in the bathroom best when I'm all by myself. When I'm alone, I can pretend it's not actually the girls' room, and instead it's just a nice place to sit and relax. I take out my silly headband and have my own locked door. I rest my elbows on my binder and read the notes people have left behind on the wall. To be honest, I thought about using a big marker to leave the girls a message there. I'm just not sure what permanent thing I would want to say. It's funny to think that my BFFs and I used to write things out of invisible ink for fun. We would play Inspector Gadget and solve cereal box mysteries together, and now I can't even leave a clue to tell them that I'm still alive and still want to be their friend.

All summer long I have been feeling far away from them, like when I offered to play Uncle Jesse in our game of *Full House* and they said that was weird for me to play the boy part. But we haven't been real friends ever since that slumber party. Don't tell anyone this, but I think it's because I said another thing that I shouldn't have. I told everyone that I think that Sofie Gavia is cute. I didn't mean to. I thought truth or dare was supposed to be a fun game. But when Sofie came back to the party from the bathroom, all the girls laughed at her because she didn't know about the bad thing I said about her. Courtney got out her parents' camcorder and said, "We have to protect Sofie from Ellie." Everybody had to listen to her because she was the birthday girl. They turned up that song "Man! I Feel Like a Woman" on the boom box, and filmed themselves building a moat of pillows and VHS tapes around Sofie's sleeping bag. Sofie just watched all confused.

I hate to admit it, but no one wanted to sleep next to me that night. They didn't want me under the backyard trampoline the next morning either. I can't write about any of this in a bathroom stall that only has hearts with people's initials inside. I don't have anyone's name to put into a heart with mine. I hope I'm not a loser and that nobody in the world sees that video Courtney made. I don't know. Things will be all right by December. Every year, Mary has a big McDonald's dinner and slumber party to celebrate both Christmas and her birthday. Mary knows I don't even need to stand on phonebooks to reach the high shelf with all of the secret sugary snacks and Christmas presents. Plus, I'm sure they all remember that I come up with the very best dares. For example, last year, I got the other girls to pee into Dixie cups in the laundry room.

This year, I dared myself to see how long I can go without speaking. I've started calling it the no talking game. Do you ever play it? I wish I'd started it sooner. It's keeping me out of trouble, and usually it's enough to just nod my head yes or no. To be very honest with you, I'm almost glad that I don't know you, because that's one less slumber party invitation I have to worry about. Maybe I wouldn't want to talk to you out loud either. No offense. That's just how I am, I guess.

I have to tell you something, though, and you have to swear on your life that you won't tell anybody. Today I stayed in my favorite bathroom stall not only through lunch, but also math class. I still think of myself as a good student, though. My mom made me do Brain Quest flash cards all summer long and my grades are almost good enough to be offered a special hall monitor job. I did my own version of math class anyways by counting all the ceiling, floor, and wall tiles. I lost count at number seventeen and got antsy when I heard the sink water running all of a sudden. I tried to hide my breath and tuck up my feet so that person would think that they were all alone. But that sink kept on going for nearly five minutes, it really seemed like enough water to take a shower or set a ship to sail. The water kept running and running, and my legs got so tired from trying to stay small. I couldn't take it anymore, and put my feet down.

I peeked under the door. Turns out, it was just Sofie. I recognized her see-through sandals. She cleared her throat and said, "Are you okay?" She turned the water off and waited for me to say something back. I took my time to turn the silver handle and let the door swing open. I was surprised Sofie waited long enough for me to come out. She stood there smiling without any teeth showing. It was impossible to ignore her.

Right then and there, we decided to start our own club for working on our confident walks in and out of the bathroom stalls. It's a super-small club with just the two of us, but that's okay. It's probably best nobody else knows about it, so it's actually a secret club. Just so you know, the secret club was Sofie's idea and it wouldn't be weird for people to see us together in the bathroom because everybody has to go in there eventually. I don't know. Do you belong to any clubs during school or maybe after school? I heard that there will be even more clubs to choose from in middle school. Anyways, I think this secret club with Sofie G could be a good thing.

Maybe when we practice our confident walks in the future, Sofie and I can use the loud hand driers to make loud noises like a very excited audience. We will clap for each other too because we can, just like the invisible studio audiences on *Boy Meets World*. What do you think? It's not like she really knows what I said about her during truth or dare anyways, right? The fact is Sofie and I have actually known each other for a long time. All the girls in our class used to get invited to all the same birthday parties. That was back when everyone called everyone a friend. There's nothing wrong with calling someone cute, I think. I hope you don't think

I'm weird for writing that. I almost crossed it out, but then I didn't. Sorry. Anyways, thanks for listening.

Bye,
Ellie

PS, Sorry, what do you think about the name Alex? Or maybe Tanya?

Friday, September 19, 1997

Dear Friend,

I just turned ten years old, which is a big deal I guess because it's two numbers and I get an allowance now. But it can be stressful to have a beginning of the school year birthday because there are so many beginnings at once. Honestly, I don't like my birthday so much. People ask me all kinds of big questions about life and call me "birthday girl" over and over again. Do you like it when people call you a girl or a boy over and over again? They always expect me to smile about it, but I would rather celebrate other things instead of being a birthday girl. I would like to celebrate the caterpillar that somehow survived the playground jungle gym last winter. I would like to celebrate my confident walk when I eventually get it down. I would like to celebrate the ice cream truck driver's birthday, which actually should be a big national holiday.

Actually, I did like my eighth birthday, back when everyone thought I was interesting in a good way. We moved all the way to Houghton because my parents needed new jobs. Even though life was a lot harder without money, Mom and Dad wanted to impress everyone by filling the whole house with streamers of every color and lucky for them, they got the whole thing on their camcorder. That party was actually the last time my whole entire basement was filled with all the girls from class. We half watched *Grease,* and took turns connecting our freckles together with the glittery gel pens I got as a present.

Sofie was at that party too. Don't tell anybody this, but I remember she reached for my hand below the table just as I was about to blow out those eight butterfly-shaped candles. And she held on hard. Do you have small things that you can't forget? Even if there were no words and it's probably not even on camera? I'm not sure why I remember that moment so much. I do think that holding hands with somebody can make everything feel bigger inside, which means more room for a bigger wish. That was the first year I blew out all of my candles at once.

My birthday this year started with my favorite pencil, with

the most fun eraser, snapping all the way in half. The tip was shaped like a happy-looking dog with big blue eyes, and it flew right out of my hand because I was trying to erase on my spelling pretest too hard. Then Dylan Beaman accidentally stepped on my favorite pencil while getting out of his chair. I guess he wanted to get to recess fast. I can't really blame him for that, can I? Maybe it was my fault for dropping it.

Dylan Beaman saw the look on my face and said, "Sorry, Ellie." I believed him. He walked away and I picked up the sharpened half of my pencil from the dusty floor. It's only about one inch long now, and won't be very helpful for erasing anymore. I decided to turn in my pretest with that spelling word half-gone and followed Dylan out to the playground.

Recess is usually my favorite time of the day too, another thing that Dylan and I have in common. All the fifth graders were playing a new game called Red Rover, and we even let some innocent fourth graders play too. Sofie and I held hands for the second time ever, but I promise you that it wasn't a big deal because she was right next to me and everybody was doing it. Everybody then shouted the words *Red Rover, Red Rover* together, and held on for dear, dear life.

I really hope this isn't true, but I think Courtney and them have figured out that Sofie and I have a secret club, because people kept trying to break us apart during Red Rover. Not even the smallest of all my old friends, Mary, was afraid of us. She kicked the dirt back for an extra-strong start, and came running toward us with a huff and puff. I felt Sofie's nails digging into my skin. We swung our arms together. It was as hard as I could hold, and guess what? We didn't break up. Instead, Mary bounced off of us like a slingshot. I couldn't help but celebrate with a tiny dance because I realized that maybe I am stronger than I know. Has that happened to you before? They thought the two of us would be weak and easy to smash in between because we usually get picked last in gym class and because I did such a bad job leading the stretches the other day. They were wrong, though.

But, I don't know, do you think I look weak? I guess you wouldn't know because we've never actually met before. I drew you a picture so you can see. I didn't include my head because I don't really like my haircut right now. Luckily, I do know how to draw a good tie-dyed shirt.

I have to admit, though, I let go of Sofie's hand on purpose when Dylan Beaman came running through. His truck-themed sweatshirt pushed against my arm, and he crashed into the grass behind us. I like to think of it as a really fast hug, our first hug actually.

I know it was wrong to let the other team get a point like that. I just wanted the small chance to be picked for Dylan's side. But instead, he chose somebody with stretchy pants that had the words *All Star* written on the butt. I gave her the stink eye, but maybe that was kind of mean of me. I really can't stop thinking about it.

At the end of recess, we all walked down the slope toward the school building and I was feeling kind of bad about the whole thing. That's when Sofie told me, "You were really strong today." It was our first talking outside of the bathroom stalls that year. I just shook my head because I didn't believe her.

This is just between you and me, but at lunch that day I decided to give Sofie an invitation to my birthday party. I don't know why, especially after what happened at that last slumber party, but I did. Sofie looked at the blue singing whale I drew on the card, and told me, "I love it." It took a few minutes of repeating her words in my head, but I finally believed her. Her smile made the lunch room feel quiet, no burps or laughs or anything. She RSVP'ed right away too. She said, "I wouldn't miss it for the world," and wrote *BIRTHDAY PARTY* on her hand in blue glitter gel pen so she wouldn't forget to come. The two of us didn't say much after that, but I put the rest of my gel pens between us to share.

I wanted to make another invitation for Dylan Beaman too, but I'm pretty sure he goes to basketball practice or something like that after school. He's probably too busy to come anyway. He always looks busy, especially when he's talking to his burping contest friends or folding paper footballs during class. I wonder what it would be like to hold Dylan Beaman's hand during Red Rover or just because. I wonder what his family is like and if he would ever want to share more than chips with me.

Sorry. I hope you're not embarrassed reading this letter, because honestly nothing is more embarrassing than thinking and writing it. I mean, why do you think I send out these balloons instead of keeping a diary? I can't have these thoughts just laying around for anybody to find.

Even though I didn't give Dylan Beaman an invite, I tried my very best to be excited about my birthday party while at school today. I looked at the clock for most of the day and even reminded Sofie about it at recess. I guess I didn't really need to remind Sofie because BIRTHDAY PARTY was still written on her hand. We were under the same maple tree where Courtney, Mary, Gina, and I used to share our secrets with each other. I felt brave being back there. Don't tell anyone this, but it was actually more fun than ever before. It was mine and Sofie's first real recess together and I didn't even pick up any daisies to ask, "He loves me? He loves me not?" Instead I made sure nobody was watching and said, "Sofie, can you tell me more about your life?"

Sofie told me that her old best friends were twins, who

loved pretending they were Mary Kate and Ashley Olsen. But then they had to move all the way to Marquette, so their dad could help build an airport where the army base used to be. Sofie also explained her dad's logging job. In the cold months, he cuts down trees so they can go to the chipper for paper and tissues to get made. Then when it's warm, he actually paints houses and does whatever people need. She even said, "I love Papa," and smiled with her head in the little daisies. I think that's so cool that she loves her family like that.

We then pretended that we were loggers too. Of course, we didn't have a chain saw for tree cutting at school, so we tried to lift the maple by circling it with our arms. Sofie's palms felt warm and sweaty. It was our third time ever holding hands. It was really the only way we could take on a tree like that. You should have seen it. My arms were a little shaky, but we did get a few of the leaves to fall.

Before anything real could happen, one of the recess aids blew her horrible whistle. I can't believe she saw us. We weren't even in actual trouble. I've been way more scared other times in my life. Do you know what I mean? The aid walked fast toward the little forest and shouted, "I can't believe this" at least three times. She hates it when we horseplay and do things she doesn't understand. Sofie and I raised our arms and stepped back like they do in those cop shows when the police say that everything we say can be used against us. I looked back at my old BFFs, who were talking in the distance.

Luckily, they were too busy talking to the kid who deals Pokémon cards to notice. I'm sure I didn't ruin my chances of getting invited to Mary's birthday party.

But I have to tell you something. I hope you don't get mad. It has been bothering me since I first mentioned it. The truth is that I technically didn't have a birthday party planned this year. I just didn't want to face the fact that Sofie would probably be the only person in the whole entire world who would say yes to my invitation.

Instead of an actual party after school today, Sofie and I took extra pipe cleaners from the art room to make glasses, kind of like the *Men in Black* alien disguises. After that, we hid quietly in the fifth graders' bathroom until all the other kids left school and the halls were totally empty. Finally, we walked a super-duper long way home.

We took a left on Military Road toward Mont Ripley, then a right, and then I took a minute to peek under the WELCOME TO HOUGHTON sign for letters while Sofie watched a small ship go by. Nothing was there waiting for me. I tried not to think about it too much as we crossed all the pretty university houses with funny Greek letters on them. We did maybe two TV shows worth of walking down that road to get to the forest of tall, skinny trees.

We mostly stayed quiet and kept on walking until we eventually found a path to the lake that didn't have any scary NO TRESPASSING signs or empty vacation houses. There was nobody to watch us as we stepped into the tall grass and took off our itchy pipe cleaner disguises.

Sofie whispered, "This is the best birthday party ever," when we finally got first sight of the water. I was so surprised she said that, I just stood there.

Sofie lifted her arms into the air until she was the same height as the tallest grass. Her tropical dress matched so nice that it looked like she grew out of the ground. She danced with the wind and the seagulls played along as they flew home, their wings hitting the air with a "swish-swish." The last of summer's dragonflies said goodbye. The song came from above, below, and places I have never been. I folded my pipe-cleaner glasses into my palms and lost track of my breathing. I hope it's okay that I'm saying this.

I'm not sure how many wishes I'm supposed to get for my birthday, but in that moment with Sofie I decided this is going to be the year I wish for more. Maybe one day I'll get brave enough to tell you what those wishes are. For now, maybe we can play this game I made up a long time ago. In this game, you call me Charlie or Sean. Alison could work too. My old friends didn't like playing this so much, but I think it could be fun to try again.

Also, I know that I mentioned that whoever finds my balloons should leave letters to me underneath the WELCOME TO HOUGHTON sign, but it would also be nice if I found a letter at that lake we went to this afternoon. I don't go there much because it feels so far away sometimes, but still. It's called Portage Lake and it's kind of shaped like a peanut. Just make sure you don't send anything to Lake Superior. There are nice agate rocks there and coal ships fun to watch, but it's just way too big to possibly find anything at all.

Sincerely,
Charlie Beck

Thursday, September 25, 1997

Dear Whoever Is Reading This,

I hope you're having a good day. Today was Picture Day and it was actually the first time I could really notice my own growth, and not just in a height way. I put my hair into a braid without any help and picked out my own outfit. I even tied a silly first grader's shoes for him.

My mom says I have enough clothes to choke a horse, but she always wants me to wear the same old bunny sweater and purple headband. I like bunnies and all, but you should know that it's just not me and it never has been. So this morning, I told Mom that I accidentally lost both of them as soon as she opened my bedroom door. She crossed her arms when she saw me in my light green flannel instead. Mom said, "You can't go to school looking like a ragamuffin." I still don't know what that means, but I said "Okay, then I can change" to make her go away.

Of course, I didn't change. She doesn't know that yet, though. And you have to cross your heart, hope to die, stick a needle in your eye, promise that you won't tell anyone. It felt good to pretend that the sweater and headband went missing even though I actually know exactly where they are. They're in my bottom dresser drawer, where also I keep my Rapunzel Barbie, old friendship bracelets, and the other things I pretend to lose. If we actually knew each other, I would just give them to you so my mom would never find them again.

Dad didn't have anything to say about my outfit when I left the house because he was sleeping on the couch. That's fine with me. I thought I looked great. That flannel shirt I chose for myself had nice white buttons and matched my tennis shoes just right, and the school gave us all free combs. We have more combs than textbooks I think. Some volunteer mom in a D.A.R.E. shirt gave them to us while we waited in line for the photographer, so we could look extra nice for Picture Day. Even so, I've decided already that I don't want to share my picture with anyone when we get them back in a few weeks.

I know that I had my favorite flannel outfit, but my long

hair makes me feel funny in a bad way. It's just not how I want people to remember me. That's why I tied my hair back into a braid to help me forget about it. Are you trying to forget about anything? Is it working for you? I'm just hoping that the D.A.R.E. mom doesn't know my mom. I don't want her telling on me for not looking "my best."

I really wanted to put away that free comb that lady gave me, but my pants pockets were sewn shut. I will never understand why someone would make a decoration pocket. It seemed like I was there forever, standing with my dang comb while that lady helped the girls straighten their French braids and butterfly clips. The line for photos barely moved, and it wrapped all the way around and down the longest hallway at school. I tried to pass time by watching the boys make airplanes and swords with their special Picture Day combs. And meanwhile, two of the boys showed their Pokémon cards out in the open. It's one thing to talk to the Pokémon dealer at recess, it's another thing to bring it into the hallways, because the school principal calls it gambling. They actually had those shiny, holographic cards that you can't even buy from vending machines. It was amazing.

One of the boys said, "Pokémon are stupid because they only know how to say their names." If anything, I think it means that they are very smart because they know themselves so well. I don't think he deserves to take care of those Pokémon. I should have expected it, though, because these are the same boys who spell teenage words into the school calculators. I wanted to say something about them breaking the rules, but I didn't. Instead, I just counted the bricks on the wall. I know for a fact that one day all of their Pokémon will transform into something that will scare them, and I can't wait for that day.

Anyways, they put the cards away fast when our teacher came out of nowhere. Mr. B put a peace sign in the air to make us all hush. His beard and white shirt looked really nice for the special day. His teeth even sparkled as we all got quiet for his big speech. A normal teacher would have just reminded us to put our names on the forms to make the line go faster, but not Mr. B. Instead of saying "cheese" to the photographer lady, he said, "Take a moment to thank yourselves for being here, for showing up, before the camera snaps." I don't know where he gets all of these ideas. I don't really know who I am, so how the heck am I supposed to thank myself?

I wonder what Dylan Beaman thought of Mr. B's speech. He was scratching his chin right next to me in line because of our last names in the alphabet. I also noticed that, even though he's a boy, he actually wanted to look nice and used his free comb from the D.A.R.E. lady. As soon as he got it, he brushed stray pieces of his hair behind his ears. I wonder how easy it is for him to thank himself for being somewhere just like Mr. B said. I hope Dylan knows that pictures are probably going to come out great with his new FORD: BUILT TOUGH T-shirt. His parents will probably want to put them into gold frames for everyone to see. If he happens to give me one of the prints, I swear on my life I won't ever give it away.

I don't know why, but after Mr. B's big speech, I actually decided to give Dylan Beaman my free comb. I kept my eyes down, and just said to him, "Here, take this." It's really the most words I've ever said to Dylan Beaman out loud. I thought that the comb would give him a reason to think about me, but the fact is that it ended up in the trash can only two minutes later. I saw him throw my comb there real quick when I bent down to double-knot my shoelaces. It seemed like a lot of other people's combs ended up in there too, so I can't take it too personal, right? A small pile of them covered the whole top layer of the big gray bin. I pretended that I didn't see what he did, and then stood back up and wiped the dust off of my knees. In that moment, though, I had a sudden feeling of losing something.

My hair tie had fallen out and my braid was coming undone. I decided to have a bathroom meeting with Sofie ASAP, which stands for as soon as possible.

This morning was my first time making a really good braid all by myself. I was so nervous that I would never be able to do it like that ever again. Do you know that feeling? I tried not to have a cow, but it really was an emergency. We aren't allowed to have walkie-talkies at school, so I signaled for Sofie using a new secret code we came up with the other day. I knocked the air three times like there was an invisible door. She knocked back.

We went to the girls' room right away and sat in two stalls right next to each other. I really didn't want her to see me struggle to fix my hair. I decided to do a basic ponytail, but for some reason I couldn't get all my hair to fit through the band. I tried over and over. On my sixth try, the little pink tie flew right out of my hands. I must have stretched it too far. It landed into the toilet without making a sound. I looked down, and I couldn't believe it. The hair tie just floated in the water like a lifesaver that I will never get to use. Of course, I had to leave it there for good. In that moment, the bathroom stall seemed smaller than ever. I don't know.

My hair squiggled everywhere, and I didn't even have my silly comb to fix it. But, for Pete's sake, why would I comb and pay attention to something I don't even like? Everybody says my hair makes me look more like Mom, but I don't want to grow up to be Mom. I held my own hands, feeling sillier than ever for hiding in the girls' room of all places.

Do you think I'm stupid? I just wanted to tie myself to a balloon and fly away, skipping Picture Day altogether.

Then out of the blue, Sofie said, "I don't know why they give us all the same kind of comb if we all have different kinds of hair. I pretended to lose my comb. I couldn't even use it." I bet you Sofie's comb is in the same trash can where Dylan Beaman threw mine. Sofie's hair is curly and today it was in many braids that her dad made really nice for Picture Day. Sofie said that when she grows up, she's not going to make her kid have the same hair as everybody else at school. It made me smile to think about her future life, even though it's probably not going to be like my life at all.

I asked Sofie through the wall, "So, what do you want to be when you grow up? Is it hard for you to know?"

Sofie said, "I don't really know anybody who does what I want to, but I think it could happen anyways." I hope she's right. I haven't told anyone this before, but I want to grow up to be a mailman or something that will involve secret gifts or me walking by myself for a long time. Maybe I could even grow up to be like Steve Irwin, that Crocodile Hunter on TV. I do like animals. Sofie wants to go to outer space or be a dancer. If she goes to the moon sometime, I hope she takes me with her and her future daughter with really cool hair. Maybe you think that's weird, but I think it could be good.

Anyways, Sofie and I left the stalls and fixed our hair in separate mirrors. I wasn't sure if my fingers could fix much. I could hardly brush through once without getting stopped by a knot. I tried to remember how much I liked my outfit, but even that seemed hard to do while looking at my reflection. I decided to be brave and offer Sofie a high five anyways. I wanted her to know that I think she looked great in her blue sparkly shirt. For the record, that is different from calling someone cute.

I guess I'll go to sleep now. I haven't really been checking under the WELCOME TO HOUGHTON sign for letters this week, but I'll try sometime soon.

Sincerely,
Charlie or Sean

Sunday, September 28, 1997

Hi,

I don't want to say too much about this, but my bedroom is pink. It's a problem with me even though I really do like flowers and cotton candy. My parents painted my room pink when we moved in, but I have felt like a boy long before that. They just don't get it. Lately, my dad has been calling it my "big-girl room" almost every time he walks in. I hardly ever talked about him to my old friends because my dad can be hard to predict. I've never even told Sofie about him because she has a really nice dad, and probably wouldn't understand.

My dad used to have a job with a bunch of other dads mining copper out of the ground in White Pine, the city where we used to live. They all say that, back in the day, our old city was the best and easiest place in the world to find a job. Then things changed. We had to move here so Dad could sell T-shirts that say COPPER COUNTRY STRONG at a small store that only plays country music and hockey games on the radio. I don't actually know what he used to do other than look for shiny things underground, but he can't do it anymore and he's still sad about it. He and his old work friends all still do things together, though, but it's not work. He calls it "hanging with the boys," and he sometimes comes home very sloppy. It makes me wonder what it means to be a boy. Do you think I would have what it takes to be a good one?

Last night was Dad's birthday and he went to "hang with the boys" at his favorite place called Dave's. It's far enough away from the university to have no students, but he says it has fun things like a pinball machine, pickled eggs, and popcorn, which is good because he likes to say that the university people "get to have everything." When Dad finally got back home, he was a whole year older and it was very dark. He stood around in my room and then fell asleep with his face on the carpet while still wearing his jeans from the night before. It's a new thing for him, and I don't really understand it. Maybe he can tell I have been feeling extra lonely this year.

At breakfast this morning, I made myself buttery toast and my mom asked me about how Dad ended up sleeping next to my rock collection. She then said, "I hate it when he gets home so late. Birthday party or not, he knows how much I prefer morning Mass." I just shook my head and took another bite of my breakfast. I don't know why she expects me to know the answer to everything. I shake my head a lot these days.

Just so you know, there are actually some really good things that happen at my house too. The best thing about my house is the basement because I used to have birthday parties there. It's now where we keep the gun cabinet, fishing poles, and all the extra boxes. Boxes are cool because they can also get sent away to places I have never been to. We have shoe boxes, package boxes, microwave boxes, and a few kind of broken boxes without labels. I like to step inside of them and pretend they are time machines or Harry Potter's closet. Some people at school might think that I'm silly if they knew I do this, but it helps me feel better.

After today's breakfast, I brought my quilt down to the basement to nap in one of the big huge boxes that the refrigerator came in. I closed the cardboard lid and even punched a bunch of little holes around the top using a pen to let the smallest amounts of light come through. From inside the box, it looked like a full galaxy close enough to touch. I just hope I don't grow any bigger. I want to always be able to fit into one of my favorite places, but lately it hurts to stay small inside a closed box for too long. I don't know. Where do you go to hide? It's okay if you don't want to tell me. I usually don't tell anyone this stuff either. If you want, maybe you can hide this letter after you find it?

I woke up from my nap with an achy back, my legs curled up next to my chest. Every part of my body cracked trying to say "good morning." I gave myself a pep talk in my head and climbed out of the cardboard box for a do-over. For the second time that day, I went to the kitchen to cook my own butter toast. I made the bread perfectly brown, put it on a nice yellow plate, and then brought it to my room to eat and play pretend with the dog next door.

The golden retriever who lives next door is the second-best thing about my house. They say at church to "Love your neighbor," and I do. I really do. My family used to have a dog that would sleep at my feet. In our kitchen, we actually still have an inspirational sign that says: YOU'RE NOT REALLY DRINKING ALONE IF YOUR DOG IS HOME. Our dog, Bean, has been dead a few years now, but we still have that sign for some reason. Anyways, Bean was a hard-nosed dog, but he was clumsy enough to trip on a stripe on the rug. Now I pretend that the doggie outside the window is mine. I'm not sure if it's a boy or a girl, but that dog is named Jax. I think it's a nice name anyways.

This afternoon, I fed Jax an invisible bite of my toast through the air, and then we both squished our noses against the cold glass. Sometimes I wish the two of us could watch movies together on the weekends. It's bad to think this, but I've thought about stealing Jax so we could live together. I would feel bad, though. Jax's mom seems nice from what I can tell. She has really, super-long hair like my Rapunzel Barbie, her bedroom has nice yellow curtains, and she always makes her kids say hi to me.

I think that things would be a little better if I also had a dog or a yellow bedroom. I don't know. I need a change or an even bigger box. Do you know what I mean?

Sincerely,
Ellie

PS, Do you believe in God? I don't really care what your answer is. It's just, I don't know. I hope it's okay I asked you that. I don't really expect anybody to write me back anymore, but writing all of this down sure does help. I would like to keep doing it if it's okay with you.

Anyways, good night.

Friday, October 3, 1997

Hello Out There,

I did a good job on my chores this week, and really earned

43

my dollar allowance. I washed dishes that weren't even mine. I picked up the American flag in front of our house after the wind knocked it down. I made my bed really nice even though literally everything was on the floor when I woke up. I don't mean to complain, but doesn't Dad know that Beanie Babies are expensive? You can't just throw them around like that. I wish I could tell someone the truth about how bad he makes me feel, especially lately.

Promise not to tell anybody this? But he has been coming in my room more and more since his birthday. He says this is just a part of life, but I don't know. He also said it's good that I'm not like other girls. I'm special. It's true I've never really thought about myself as a girl, so maybe what he is saying is right. He just loves me more than before. Sorry, I don't really want to talk about this anymore.

To be honest, I haven't said a word out loud for the past few recesses and I don't feel proud of myself for doing so good at my no talking game. Maybe life will be better when I'm a grown-up. All week long, Sofie and I have been sitting next to that giant rock on the playground just waiting for time to pass. I bet that rock is so heavy that it would take a big storm for it to blow away. Thank goodness that hasn't happened yet. My dad says, "The whole state of Michigan is riding out a storm with this economy." I wonder if Sofie's dad ever says the same things as he does. Either way, the big rock gives me and Sofie a nice place to rest our backs and watch the wind push the leaves around. Nobody can tattletale on us for just sitting quiet next to each other, people get in way bigger trouble for trying to jump off of that rock like a cliff.

The last time Sofie asked me "How are you?" I didn't want to say too much of the wrong thing. I don't want to get in the way of whatever anybody might want. I shook my head and bunched up my toes, so I took up a half an inch less of space. She kept her eyes to the playground and buttoned up her Tweety Bird jacket a little bit more. I wish I could have told Sofie "Thank you for sitting next to me no matter what." Instead, I just kept sitting there in silence. Do you ever have a hard time saying a nice thing?

Just before the recess bell rang, Sofie picked up a small red-brown rock and put it in her pocket. I found another red-brown rock and put it in my pocket. I came up with a new tradition. Now, every morning when Sofie walks to school without me, she walks five blocks out of the way to put a rock on my front porch. And whenever I walk home from school without Sofie, I go five blocks out of the way to put a rock on her front porch. It's just our way of saying "I'm okay" and "hello" and "thank you." If more than three days pass by without rocks on the porches or without seeing each other at all, we will know something messy or bad has happened. That way, we don't have to answer "How are you?" with words anymore.

I have started making a circle around my bed with all the

rocks she gives me. I set them almost exactly two inches away from each other to make an invisible force field. Sometimes it gets kicked over, and the rocks tumble under my bed rolling too far away to reach. Some of them I'm not so sure I will ever get back. Have you ever lost anything that you still think about? Sometimes I still think about my favorite Snow White Polly Pocket I lost in the grass a few years ago. At the time, I was so scared that she fell asleep in the wrong place. Now I think I know how she feels.

The truth is, Sofie loves her house and she really loves her family. But I leave Sofie rocks even when things are messy or bad at my house. I know that Sofie looks forward to seeing them on her porch every afternoon. I don't want to let my only friend down. I try to pick nice rocks for her with smooth surfaces and speckles that don't have matching colored pencils. Really nice rocks come from Misery Bay, and really, really nice ones come from Marquette when my family used to go watch the ships carry iron away. Lately, I just stick to finding ones in my own neighborhood and always keep a few in my jacket pockets just in case. I think they are helping.

Sofie and I sat at the giant rock again at recess today. We watched the clouds move slowly and gently until they changed completely. A plane eventually flew by. For a moment, I imagined someone reaching out the window and catching one of my balloon letters from the inside. But it just kept flying away until it was in somebody else's sky. I tried my best not to feel left behind by whoever was in there.

I looked to my side to see if Sofie saw what I saw, but her eyes were closed. She was sound asleep. I wonder what she was dreaming about. A small snore blew between the gaps of her new adult teeth. Our recess rock's shadow made a blue blanket over her whole entire body. For a moment, it felt even bigger than the sky. I inched into my own corner of the shadow and decided to try closing my eyes too.

I have to ask, is anyone watching over me? Over us? The priest at my church always likes to say "The Lord is a rock." I think he is right about that. I don't always know what I believe in, but I should tell you that Sofie and I are okay when we're all the way down here next to our rock. It helps us both sleep.

Thanks for listening,
Paul

Tuesday, October 7, 1997

Hi,

I saw Sofie's dad at the store when I got my balloon today. Just so you know, he looks nothing like my dad. He's much shorter, has darker skin, and a smile. The new lady working there was giving him funny looks while he was trying to pick out the right air freshener for his logging truck. I have a hard time deciding on things too, but that lady kept asking him "Can I help you with anything, sir?" over and over again like she wanted him to hurry up and leave. Either way, he took his time and I think that's good.

I haven't actually seen Sofie's dad since the PTO cake walk last year, but I worked up the courage to walk over and say "Hi, Mr. Gavia." He said back in a deep voice, "Hi, you must be Ellie. I've heard so much about you from Sofie." He even told me that I can call him Richard from now on and maybe the three of us could all go trick-or-treating together. He is a nice man from Detroit and has a missing finger from hard work, just like my grandpa. I liked him right away. I then thought about asking Richard to buy me a Cow Tail candy, but instead I just kept my mouth shut so he wouldn't take back his Halloween invitation. I really hope it works out because Courtney and them sure as heck won't invite me for trick-or-treating this year. I don't really think things will get better over the next few weeks.

To be very honest with you, I have been feeling kind of lost lately. There were a lot of girls in the bathroom at school this morning. I just felt really out of place. Not just in a not having a lot of friends way, but in a way I can't really describe. I just tried telling myself, "You're a special girl, not like the rest," just like my dad said. But I don't know. I used to feel so sure and happy calling myself a boy. Ever since Dad started walking into my room and loving like he does, I am just feeling more afraid of boys. The other day, I even saw him punch his bedroom wall when there was nobody else to fight. He would never do that to another person. Am I supposed to be scared of myself? I don't know.

I feel so turned around. I even told myself in the bathroom stall, "You're not a boy. You can't be one." When I had that thought, I just stared at the wall.

I imagined someone taking a giant pink eraser to my whole entire body. They started with the middle to separate my parts, my heart, my gut. The rest was scrubbed away one by one, my hands, my legs, my head. Then there was nothing left with the girls' room toilet un-flushed. Have you ever felt that way before? I don't know.

Mr. B told us this morning at school, "Every time we lie to ourselves, it's like taking the wrong turn on a map." We get lost if we do it too much for too long. I just don't know, do I even have a map if I feel gone completely? But I had to try anyways because school is like that. To help us figure out our maps, we had a special class assignment where each of us had to make two lists onto giant pieces of paper. One list was supposed to be about ten things we remember, and the other about ten things we love. I'm still not sure if this assignment was really good timing or really bad timing, but I wrote something like this:

**Ten things I remember:**

I remember the Michigan state tree is the white pine.

I remember how to push myself on the swing using my own leg muscles.

I remember the sound of my old dog when he's mad about something.

I remember to turn off the porch light.

I remember to read the jokes on Popsicle sticks before throwing them away.

I remember my old address.

I remember watching our favorite show, *Boy Meets World*, at my friend Courtney's house.

I remember to write Christmas cards for my

aunts and uncles in Wisconsin even though
we hardly know each other.

I remember to put on a smile when someone
with a camera says "cheese."

I remember the Stanley Cup is actually in the
summer and not the winter.

**Ten things I love:**

I love my bedroom window.

I love my friend Sofie.

I love ice cream that turns my mouth different
colors, especially Superman ice cream and
anything made by Jilbert's.

I couldn't finish the "Ten things I love" list. I would have
said I love sleeping in my bed, but I'm not sure about that
anymore. I would have said I loved my pencil with the dog-
shaped eraser, but Dylan had to step on it. I know we have a
school store with that cool pencil machine and all, but nothing will be as good as what I had. I don't know. I don't know
why I'm saying sorry, but I'm sorry. Dylan Beaman sped
through the whole thing figuring out what he remembered
and loved in less than five minutes. He was one of the first
people to put it in Mr. B's wire basket.

I felt further away from a good answer every time I
watched another classmate walk to the front of the room.

I felt so far away from everything. For the second time that day, I imagined the giant pink eraser taking me away. I had to snap out of it because soon I was the only one left who hadn't turned in the assignment. Everyone was looking so bored waiting for me to figure it out, and the clock ticking in the corner was not helping. Some kids even started talking to each other like they had forgotten about me. Couldn't they see that I was still working? That I'm still here even when I don't want to be? I have never felt my face get so warm and pink from embarrassment. I'm surprised I didn't ball up my piece of paper completely.

For some reason, I got scared by the love list. So instead of writing down ten things like I was supposed to, I last-minute decided to draw a picture of Saturn. I read that Saturn always has a storm on it, but somehow all the rings of rocks hold it together. Maybe it's stupid, but I hope Mr. B understands.

After I finished shading in the planet, I walked in front of the whole class to finally turn in my lists. At that point, the bell had already rung. Courtney blew a bubble with her Spice Girls gum because she was so bored. I didn't even think gum was allowed at school. I crossed my arms and went back to my desk, my least confident walk yet. My page was half-empty, but I still feel like I shared too much of myself. I hope I didn't share too much of myself with you either. I'm sorry.

I don't really have anything else to say, so I drew you the

whole entire solar system above. If you want, you can tell me about the things that you love or remember.

Sincerely,
Ellie Beck

Hi.

I hope you like this balloon. In case you happened to find and read any of my recent balloon letters, you can just ignore them. I'm fine now. Today was very nice for the most part.

Dylan Beaman offered me another potato chip at lunch. It was extra yellow and extra salty, and it made me so happy. After that, Sofie and I skipped confident walk practice to talk about cool Halloween costumes that nobody will recognize us in. We'll see how that goes if I only have pipe cleaners and tinfoil to make something good, but we've got good imaginations.

In other news, I actually heard a rumor at school that my old friend Mary said that Gina said that Courtney said that she is cousins with that singer Leanne Rimes. Maybe Courtney has a good imagination too, but I can't wait to be the one to say "I told you so" when everybody realizes her story isn't true.

Also, when I got home from school, there was a special about Princess Diana on TV. People got into her face with cameras, just like what happened in the last episode of *Boy Meets World*. It's too bad Princess Diana actually died, though. I think my mom even cried about it. I wonder what it's like to have so many people cry about you. I wonder what it's like to have the whole world want to see you and take your picture. Just between you and me, I actually got my Picture Day pictures back. I think I get what my mom meant by "ragamuffin." My hair was all wrong and my face is weird, and I know for a fact that my family won't be happy to see me in my flannel. All this to say that it's best that nobody else knows about those photos for now.

Sincerely,
Me

Wednesday, October 15, 1997

Hi,

I'm skipping chocolate milk this week to write a second letter with my allowance money. Mom is mad and tired about something right now. I hope it has nothing to do with me. Dad keeps shouting "I'm doing my best" and "You should try being me." He yells a lot when they're alone together downstairs and he is so quiet when he is alone with me upstairs.

I've even said a prayer asking for all of it to stop. I keep wanting things to just be fine. It hasn't worked yet.

I wish my biggest problem was still getting to play Uncle Jesse in a game of *Full House* with my old friends. But it's not. I'm so tired and I'm so hungry right now, but I really don't want to go downstairs to look for food. As Uncle Jesse would say, "Lord, have mercy." I know God doesn't work this way, but I also said a prayer for a cheese pizza to somehow appear in my room.

I have another prayer too. If that's not too expensive, maybe you or somebody out there could write something nice about me for *The Daily Mining Gazette* Sweetest Day announcements? It's only three days away, and I promise that I will read it and I will be grateful. If you do it, I will even find a way to pay you back. I promise.

I don't know, I'm sorry. Some good news is that it snowed two inches over the raked leaves yesterday. It gives me something nice to look at outside my window. Also, Halloween with Sofie and her dad is only fifteen days away.

Hope you're okay. I'm doing my best.

Sincerely,
Ellie Beck


PS, Sorry, I'm still awake because downstairs is still so noisy. I'm just wondering, have you ever seen the *Jerry*

*Springer Show*? Well, I'm just wondering why does everyone say Jerry's name over and over again when people are fighting on the show? Do you think he got to pick his own name? Do you think he gets tired of hearing people yell all the time? I'm not so sure. I guess I can see how it's my dad's second-favorite show. A lot of people on that show have probably hit their walls too.

Anyways, I should go now. Good night.

Ellie

Sunday, October 19, 1997

Dear Friend,

Dad actually threw away his *Daily Mining Gazette* before I had a chance to read any Sweetest Day announcements, so I'm really sorry if you or anybody else tried to do something nice for me. Maybe that's what I get for asking. Anyways, I went to church today with Mom and Dad. That probably counts for something.

Dad saw his old work friend, who was wearing nice pants and a belt, at the service. That man has a new job at that mining museum my old Girl Scouts troop went to once. Dad sure had a lot to say about that in the car ride home. He even called his friend a traitor and some other words I'm not going to say right now. Anyways, it was good timing because the priest made a speech today about the difference between "hot-blooded" and "cold-blooded" people. One means good and one means bad, but I can't remember which one is which. Now that I think about it, it's weird because everyone has blood inside of them.

We go to church every Sunday because Mom and Dad want people to see them there holding hands, but it's actually an easy place to hide. Today I asked Mom if I could go to the bathroom. I didn't really have to go. I mostly just wanted to do my own thing. I don't think God minds that much because I'm at least looking at the nice art in the hallway.

I took my time walking four laps around the building. After that, I actually did have to pee. Don't tell anyone, but I think I figured out how to pee standing up. Surprisingly enough, wearing a skirt made it much easier. I wish I had known that a few years ago when I first started practicing. All I had to do was just bend my knees a little bit. It was cool. It was the best part of the day actually. I will probably try again soon, probably the next time Mom makes me wear a dress.

When I got back to the chapel, it was time to eat the fake bread. My parents then went to "make confession," where they tell the priest secrets in a tiny wooden room. Even if Mom and Dad told me to, I wouldn't ever tell that man anything, not even the best part of my day. It's not that he's a bad person or anything. I don't know, it's just that why would I want to be in a small room with some man? I don't like that at all.

Maybe it's a sin, but I wonder what Dad tells the priest because Dad almost always says what he's thinking. For example, on the car ride home this afternoon, he told Mom that she's too fat and her hair looks too much like "a boy's haircut." He thinks she should look more like Shania Twain. He said, "You could really be beautiful if you tried a little bit harder." Mom just nodded her head. I would have done the same thing if I were her. I always just nod my head when he gives me weird compliments.

Actually Dad might have one secret. Don't tell anyone this, but I saw him crying in the backyard a few days ago. At that point, he had probably shouted "I'm doing my best" at Mom twenty times. The ice on the branches above made it look like it was just snowing on top of his head. He bent himself into a ball, barely shivering in his COPPER COUNTRY STRONG T-shirt. What does it mean when the thing that is supposed to make us strong isn't here like it used to be?

I don't know. I would never call Dad a crybaby, though. I have never actually seen another boy cry before in my entire life. I don't think it's about being hot-blooded or cold-blooded.

I have to ask, do you think of yourself as strong? Can I

still be a boy if I cry sometimes too? Can I still be a boy if I've never punched a wall before?

Sorry. I'm being weird. I'm just thinking about stuff.

Sincerely,
Alex

Friday, October 31, 1997

Dear Whoever Is Reading This,

Thank you for listening even if you don't have to. I'm sure you already know this, but today was Halloween. What were you? Have you ever been a ghost? Last year I was left-behind bubble gum, which you know can be a scary thing if you have ever stepped in some. I dressed in all pink and duct-taped a shoe to the top of my head. I liked feeling stretchy and getting to hide under tables for fun, but most people didn't get it. Some people had the nerve to say that it wasn't a real costume. I don't know why, but that still really bothers me.

After a lot of thinking, I decided to be a moth for Halloween this year since everyone has seen a moth before. Sometimes real-life ones tap on my bedroom window when

I'm home with the lights on. I think it's cool that moths can eat whole blankets and sweaters and other things I cover myself with. I made the costume all by myself this afternoon by patching together tinfoil and bright green pipe cleaners I borrowed from the art room. I stood in front of our bath-room mirror to make sure my wings were big enough and the curly antennas were just right on my head. I smiled to myself. In that moment, I thought I looked great and I had myself to thank.

It was really nice to get out of the house and, believe it or not, the weather was kind of okay for trick-or-treating too. Sofie and I unzipped our puffy coats and kept our costumes out of hiding. Do you ever have to cover something that you don't want to? It's really the worst, especially when it's some-thing that makes you happy.

I hate to admit it, but for the second year in a row most of the grown-ups I met while trick-or-treating confused me for other things. Some even gave up on guessing, and gave me one of those caramel-apple suckers anyways. I didn't know whether or not to correct them when they guessed wrong because I still wanted their candy. I guess it's okay if they didn't see that I was truly a moth as long as I knew what I was and my trick-or-treating buddies, Sofie and her dad, knew what I was too. Mr. B always says that you only have to touch one person for art to be good. It's hard to believe that right now, but deep down I know that he's right.

But for the record, I was not Tinker Bell, an angel, or a Picasso painting. I was for sure not the tooth fairy, especially when I still have some baby teeth and that would just be confusing. I worked hard to be a moth. Plus, making my own outfit really helped my confident walk while going around the block. My steps were bigger than any bathroom stall meeting ever. No one else had the exact same Halloween costume as me, and I felt memorable in a good way.

Sofie's dad even took off his *Scream* mask, which was basically a sad face melting off, just to tell me how good my outfit was. He was so impressed that I made my moth costume all by myself and he said, "Nobody can do what you do." My old BFFs' parents never said anything to me like that. The grown-ups were actually the first ones to point and make fun of my bubblegum costume when we took pictures in front of Mary's house last year. All the other kids had store-bought costumes like Helga Pataki and the Sailor Scouts.

This year, Sofie was dressed as the pop star named Selena with purple sparkly pants and a plastic microphone. Not only is Sofie going to be an astronaut and dancer when she grows up, she's going to become a singer too. She did a twirl on the sidewalk and practically shouted, "I'm going to arrive to my big concert sitting in the back of a white horse carriage, just like Selena did."

Richard smiled and said, "Then let's make a Selena horse carriage for the big winter concert, honey bug." I wasn't even looking forward to the concert, but now I am. Richard promised that I can come over to help them paint their rusty bomber car white for Sofie's grand arrival. I hope it actually happens because I love Sofie's voice and I want the world to hear it. You'll hear it one day. I have no doubt about it. I reminded Sofie that in the movie about Selena's life, the moon tells her that she can be whatever she wants to be. I try to remember that every time I look at the moon now. I try to remember that even Selena was a little girl once too.

Without even thinking, I grabbed Sofie's hand and said, "We have to make it to the moon before we die." Sofie lit up, and I could have sworn that I saw the moon shining in the distance all of a sudden. It was so clear and round that it was practically singing to us. Sofie and I ran up the dark slope toward the light, leaving Richard behind to eat a Kit Kat bar.

Turns out it wasn't moonlight. It was just a streetlamp. I felt bad about it only until Sofie held her microphone up to her lips to say "Dance with me." She started to wiggle around under the fake moon. Her orange bucket rattled with candy as she sang a song that she wrote herself, "Shake, Shake, Shake." "Shake, shake, shake" are the only words in that song, but it still totally rocks. She air-kissed the invisible audience, and I even added some of my own lyrics inspired by the movie *Good Burger*. The words go, "I'm a dude, he's a dude, she's a dude because we're all dudes." Sofie knows that song too, and it was the perfect remix. I felt our music everywhere as we shook our whole bodies. The tips of my fingers and hair came alive. *"Shake, shake, shake. I'm a dude. Shake, shake, shake. He's a dude. Shake, shake, shake. She's a dude. Shake, shake, shake. Because we're all dudes."*

It was fun at first, but my shakes and shouts made my antennas fall off, under the light, of all places. All of a sudden, who picks them up but Dylan Beaman dressed up as Batman. It was my first time ever seeing Dylan outside of school. I hope he didn't hear me say "I'm a dude." It was actually the first time Sofie and I were being seen doing anything together outside of school, and our costumes didn't exactly cover up who we actually are. We were totally busted.

Dylan stepped into the circle of light. He was there with his whole family. His little brothers were dressed as a hunters in bright orange and army colors. Their mom and dad were Houghton High School football players with black lines under their eyes. They were probably feeling super confident because Houghton kicked butt at the Copper Bowl against Hancock High this year. The Beaman family all wrinkled their noses in the exact same way when they caught me singing and dancing. Dylan Beaman handed me my neon antennas with a laugh and said, "What are you supposed to be?"

Before I could say anything back, he and his whole family walked away and disappeared down that hill. In that moment, I made a promise to myself to never sing in front of people again. Ever. I just wish I knew what the Beamans were thinking when they walked away. I hope they didn't think my confident walk was too weird. Do you think I'm weird? Maybe I take back what I said about getting excited for the winter concert.

I don't think Sofie heard what happened with Dylan. She just kept on dancing that whole entire time he was there. I waited for her to notice, but I don't know. I stopped singing and she finally paused to look at me with big eyes. I swallowed and imagined my whole voice going down with it. For the rest of the night, Sofie put her pop star microphone up to her mouth every time a grown-up asked her what kind of candy she wanted. It sounded like she really knew the answers too. I hate that I couldn't feel the same confidence anymore.

Sofie asked, "Do you want to try holding my mic?" as we left the cool-looking, purple strobe-light house. I scrunched up my nose and said, "No, thanks." I did the exact same thing when Richard sang about sharing his Kit Kat bar with me. I know the two of them didn't deserve those faces, but I was half expecting the Beaman family would show up again any minute. I hardly said anything for the rest of our trick-or-treating time. I never thought I would say this, but I just wanted to go home. I wanted to take my moth costume off as soon as possible.

I decided to go back to my house a few blocks early, I threw my wings on the floor of my room and emptied out the candy in my pillowcase into a big plastic bowl. Now I can't sleep. It's way past my bedtime and I'm thinking way too much. I don't know. Why is it I can get a whole pillow-case of candy and still get so stuck on that one look, that one laugh? It's too late to take back my singing and dancing and whatever else I did out there for Dylan and everybody in the world to see. To undo it, I think I will have to become a paper-football champion or learn how to burp out the alphabet. I might have to become really pretty somehow. Something like that, I don't know. All of these things will take way too long, though. Do you have any ideas for me?

I just know that next time I will try my very best to keep away from the light, even though that's not what a moth would do. Gosh, or maybe there will be no next time at all because middle schoolers probably can't go trick-or-treating anyways. Who knows?

Sorry, I should go to bed now. Good thing it's not a school night.

Sincerely,
Me


PS, Okay. Hi. I just came up with the perfect plan, and I am already feeling so much better. I am going to share my trick-or-treat candy with Dylan Beaman. Maybe if I pick very, very carefully what I share with him, he will think that I am cool. If Dylan Beaman thinks I'm cool, then I will for sure be invited to Mary's birthday party. Even if they don't think I'm cool, my old friends like Dylan's opinion more than their own. I'll just make sure to leave my antennas at home, maybe hide them in my drawer with all my other stuff. How does that sound? Actually, no, don't tell me. I know it's a good idea.

Good night again,
Kye

Monday, November 3, 1997

Hi,

I hope someone tells you that you are good every single day, even on days when you're feeling like you made a mistake under a streetlight or whatever. I was wishing someone told me that today. It was parent-teacher conferences and I had to go with my mom because it was also errands day.

To be honest, it was hard even before we left the house. Mom found my Picture Day pictures. She finally found them while going through my drawers. She said, "God help us" and "Ellie, you could really be beautiful if you tried a little bit harder." I just nodded my head. I know I've heard that before somewhere. Mom's worried that Dad is not gonna know what happened to his "pretty little girl." I hope she knows that she's the only one who actually calls me that. She threw my Picture Day pictures in the wastebasket. She didn't even see what name I put on my form. Afterward, Mom made me put on a purple dress and plastic headband. She put on her nice shirt from Dad's store that says MICHIGAN, THE SUPERIOR STATE in rhinestones.

I know that we don't know each other, but do you think I'm beautiful? I'm just wondering if there is anything I can do to be beautiful that doesn't mean wearing that purple thing. That dress doesn't even fit me anymore. Either way, I probably complained about it too much. Mom told me "You're being too sensitive," and gave me an animal-themed coloring book from the Dollar Tree at Copper Country Mall. Doesn't Mom know that fifth graders aren't supposed to have coloring books? I hardly touched it in the car, and instead watched her smoking lots of cigarettes through the rear-view mirror. I bet she wanted a cigarette for parent-teacher conferences too, but everybody knows there is no smoking allowed at school.

I felt like everybody noticed me and Mom when we walked into the school gym. The room was full of echoes and we had to pass by a bunch of people waiting in gray folding chairs. I sat in the farthest corner I could find as Mom got in line to talk to Mr. B. I get kind of scared when I know that people are talking about me. If parents and teachers were saying good things, you would think that they want us kids to be there for the whole conversation so we could feel good about ourselves. Now that I think about it, there should be a place for us to go review our parents. Then again, I'm not really sure what I would be allowed to say about mine.

I was so nervous that I barely looked at the coloring book while Mom stood in line. She put on her lipstick and looked around the room. She hardly waved to anyone, just a lady from church and my old Girl Scouts troop leader. The only other kid there was that quiet boy with the VH1 binder from my class. I half smiled at him to be nice. His name is Nathan Lucas. He lives all the way in Calumet, and looked just as nervous as me. I saw Mr. B smile and nod a lot while talking to his dad. Nathan Lucas must be smart even though he doesn't talk. I just crossed my fingers for Mr. B to give my mom the exact same smile.

I think I can be a good student. I think I can be good. I did great on my science test the other day. It's because we have been learning about rocks, so it's easy for me. I've also have been better about not hiding out in the bathroom stall during class, which means I get to sit next to Dylan Beaman some more.

When Mr. B finally got to my mom, he used his arms a bunch while talking. His smile was only a little bit there. Maybe he was talking about doing more group projects, or everybody needing a longer recess. Maybe they were just talking about the weather like most other grown-ups do. Truth is, I'm so bad at reading lips. I mostly just wanted to know whether or not Mr. B told Mom that I sometimes change my name on my school papers. I kind of hope that he did say something because I'm not so sure how to bring it up to her. Maybe he would be able to explain it in a better way than I could. I also kind of hope that he didn't tell her. I bet Mom thought hard about what name to give me, and she's already mad about my Picture Day pictures.

She told me this morning that the name Ellie means "beautiful" in some other language. Sometimes when people call me Ellie, I feel like a ghost. I feel like they don't see me at all. It's kind of hard to explain. It gets harder to explain every year.

I do wonder how Mr. B always knows that all those homework pages are from me. I change the name so often, but he never marks me as incomplete. Luckily, I narrowed it down to a few names, so I bet that helps, Charlie, Sawyer, Logan, and Sean, and Paul and Max and Kye, Aaron, Alex, and Alison and Lila. Even Ilona and Tanya are nice names too. Or maybe even MJ or just a C, not sure what those letters would stand for, but I think that they sound cool. I guess that's more than a few. I guess I got a lot more work to do. It's just a lot on top of schoolwork, I think. Sometimes I have trouble filling out tests when the name part feels like a test too. The name blank is always on the tippy-top of every page. It's bad.

When I write letters, I love that you have to read all of my thoughts and stories before I say any name at all. You have to make it to the very end to know.

I just really hope that Mom walked away from the gym still thinking I am good and the teacher won't ever mark me as incomplete. To be honest with you, I really wanted Mom to pat my back the same way Nathan Lucas's dad did for him. Instead, we walked out of the school and drove past so many pine trees and streetlights in silence. It's not weird for me not to say anything, but it's definitely weird for her. The radio wasn't even on. Maybe this is strange to say, but I imagined myself outside running alongside the car. That version of me is much faster at running than I am in real life.

I came back to my body all of a sudden when my mom said, "Mr. B seems like a nice man." I wish she had said more. There was another long silence that lasted until we pulled into Freedom Valu's gas station, the one next to Portage Bridge and the Houghton welcome sign. It was time for her to get the usual skim milk and bingo cards. The wind threw the car door shut. Mom locked it with me inside facing that yellow WE LOVE SERVING YOU THE VERY BEST sign. I thought about checking the Houghton welcome sign for any letters, but instead I decided to fill in a page from that coloring book Mom gave me. I was hoping that Mom would tell me "I love it" when it was all done, and then that would mean that she loves me.

The first page I opened to had a picture of a horse with a saddle and reins. I imagined the horse was secretly a unicorn, so I left the fur white and made the mane purple. The leaves in the background took longer to color than anything. I wanted to make them like fall time with a mix of yellow and orange colored pencil. I didn't get to color in the fence because Mom was already walking back with her plastic shopping bag. I ripped out the page, wrote the name Ellie as big as I could on the bottom, and slid it between the front seats. I only had six seconds left to brush my hair with my fingers.

She plopped into her seat and slammed the door shut, maybe louder than she meant to. From the backseat, I could see Mom's red polished nails pick up the secret unicorn. She put it down right where I had left it and started the engine. I know that she just looked at it for only three seconds, but I hope it made her happy.

Hope to hear from you or anybody, really.

Sincerely,
Ellie

PS, If you and I really were friends, maybe you could invite me to your birthday party? I would be really good and also do my best to make sure you have fun. I would show you my new hat from Dad's store and we could talk about deer season starting or ice skating. I don't know, it's just something to think about.

Sincerely again,
Ellie Beck

Tuesday, November 4, 1997

To Whom It May Concern:

I don't know who even writes a letter that starts like that, but in school we have been learning how to write business complaints and letters to people we don't know. This isn't a complaint, but I decided to skip chocolate milk again this week just so I have enough money to write more than one balloon letter.

Sofie, Richard, and I finally painted their car white after school today. Sofie really is going to arrive to the big winter concert in a white horse carriage, just like Selena did. To make it, we did some sanding and then covered all the car lights and windows with thick tape so they didn't get messed up. We had to wear gloves and junk shirts too. My favorite part was getting to listen to a radio station that played fast music that I never get to listen to with my parents.

After that, Mrs. Gavia let me stay for their whitefish dinner. She's a nice lady, also from Detroit. But there's a bad rumor at school that Sofie's family aren't true Yoopers because they weren't born in the Upper Peninsula. I don't know what to believe, but I will say that Mrs. Gavia knows how to clean a fish real good. I also got to meet Sofie's baby sister for the first time ever too. Her name is Viivi. She was actually born here in Houghton, so I guess those mad people can at least call her a true Yooper. She has black curly hair, the world's tiniest Big Bird overalls, and we made lots of eye contact since she doesn't know any real words yet. I have to admit, she's very cute. I kind of wish I had a brother or sister now too, so we could do things and remember things together.

Anyways, we just chilled after that. The whole family played Uno and ate raspberry coffee cake while the cat, Dusty, slept on the floor. Sofie's dad had a hard time, though, because he's actually color blind, but he still got second place. Sofie's house is so cool. It's not like mine at all. She's got a carpet and polka-dotted wallpaper in the basement, an ocean-themed bathroom without a weight scale, and a pretty painting of tree roots and branches that hangs on the front porch. I got to stay all the way until it was time for Sofie's singing lesson. She and her dad practice singing "Do-Re-Mi" over and over again at the top of their lungs. He wants to get her ready in time for the winter concert. Hold on, I'll be right back.

Sorry about that. I was just thinking about asking my parents to turn down the TV, but then I changed my mind. The last time I went downstairs to ask Dad to turn the volume down, it only got turned up to teach me a lesson. Sometimes I don't really understand what he's trying to teach me. To be honest, it's almost impossible to think with how loud the TV is sometimes. Don't get me wrong, I like my shows and all. But Mom and Dad are actually in love with that TV, especially when the Patriots are losing or it's telling the weather that will be wrong anyways. They also really like these cop shows where people shout a lot and they take away girls with skirts and blurry faces. It's weird.

Sorry. Let's talk about something else now.

Well, okay, in case you were wondering, I send out my balloon letters late at night when everyone is busy with something else. I usually get the day's balloon on my way home from school, which means I get to spend fifteen minutes less at home and fifteen minutes more all by myself, feeling like a grown-up. When I get home, I hide my balloon in the back corner of my bedroom closet. Sometimes before dinner, I check on it to make sure it is still afloat.

Most of the time, I write my letter an hour or two after dinner, when Mom thinks that I'm sleeping. After I finish my writing, I tie it to the end of my balloon with triple knots. The very, very last step is opening my window, and letting the balloon fly past my neighbors' trees and everything else in my world.

So anyways, that's all I really wanted to say. I'm going to go now and listen to that "Do-Re-Mi" song. At our last secret bathroom meeting, Sofie gave me the *Sound of Music* tape to borrow. Sometimes it's helpful to have songs ready when we practice our confident walks, especially when we want to add some cool arm moves. Last week we tried with that "What is love? Baby, don't hurt me no more" song and it was really fun. Don't worry, though, I just move my lips. I've learned from Halloween to never sing in front of anybody for as long as I live and I'm okay with that. I don't even like singing that much.

Also, guess what. Speaking of Halloween, I narrowed down what candy I want to give Dylan. It's now between Reese's, a mystery Airhead, an Extreme Sour Warhead, and little pack of Starbursts. In a dream world, I would have candy cigarettes to offer him, but I'm sure I will figure it out soon.

Later, gator,
Sawyer Beck

Hey-lo,

Things are so good right now. I almost want to write my name at the top of the page for a change, but I will save it for the end. The sun really peeked out today too. The light going through the leaves almost looked like stained glass. Some of the leaves fell onto my head as I walked to Sofie's to put a rock on her porch.

I like fall time the most of all because people find change beautiful for once. Usually they don't like change so much, like that time the news said that Dad's old copper mine might get turned into a landfill or nuclear waste zone. He threw the remote and said that the government was just using us so we could become a "theme park for other places." It's true, people do come from other parts of Michigan, and even Wisconsin, just to see our nature and leaf colors change. They take these long drives, and it's a celebration for them. They notice how the trees have changed from green to fire colors overnight, and then they leave. But it's not that simple. A lot more is changing.

I hope someone celebrates me when I change. Today I feel good, but sometimes I'm afraid of changing in the wrong

77

ways. I've been having growth spurts, and not just in my height. The things I like aren't even the same. It's not good. I don't know. I guess I shouldn't be so hard on myself, especially because I shared a Halloween candy with Dylan yesterday and it went so well. In case you were wondering, I ended up going with the Reese's. It felt a little warmer than expected when I pulled it out of my pocket. I slid it onto his desk, and crossed my fingers that the chocolate didn't melt too much. Dylan dropped the Green Bay paper football he was trying to fold, and said "Boo-yah." He ate his present right away.

Courtney and Mary turned their heads in our direction when all that happened. You should have seen Mary's face, though. She almost looked like she had the *Scream* mask on. Either way, they looked really cool in their scrunchy shirts and seashell necklaces. I bet they thought I was a little bit cool too, because just a minute later Dylan Beaman smiled at me. He showed bits of chocolate in the corners of his lips and in between his two front teeth. Dylan seemed truly excited for the first time in forever. He even looked happier than that time I got to watch him up close at that all-boys burping contest. I wanted to give him a hug with his candy, but I decided that would be a bad idea because everyone would have seen it.

Really, I had Sofie to thank for all the success because she helped me choose which candy to give Dylan. That was nice of her. She doesn't know Dylan well, but she is good at paying attention. She said, "Dylan would of course like the peanut butter candy because he has been eating peanut butter sandwiches every day ever since the first grade." That was before I moved to Houghton, so I didn't even know that.

Sofie did a really nice thing today too. During silent reading time, I was reading a book about a lost dog and I noticed Sofie rattling the pencil sharpener near my desk. She covered her mouth trying to keep the SRT rule, but I could see her giggling right through it.

I looked down and there was a Skechers' shoebox by my feet. It was filled to the very top with all of her trick-or-treat goodies that had a green wrapper. Can you believe it? She knew my favorite color is green without ever even asking me. It was like finding buried treasure without a map. All I had to do was look down, which is good because I'm not so great at following maps made by other people. I wouldn't say this at any slumber party in the history of ever, but I'll tell you. I think that Sofie is all that and a bag of chips.

At recess, the two of us dumped the shoebox onto the grass by the Secrets Tree that we couldn't chop down. Every piece of candy tumbled out of the box. I never knew there were so many shades of green. The candies were lime colored, spooky olive colored, hunting gear colored, and others were the same color as a mermaid's tail. We looked at our fortune, and Sofie said, "I want to try something."

She had me lie flat on the soft ground, and then she placed the green candies around my body like a tree getting ready to shed its leaves. She worked carefully, as if she knew where each piece belonged. Do you ever feel like you're exactly in the right place at the right time? That's how I felt. I liked listening to her quietly sing the song "MmmBop" while she placed the candies around me, the wrappers crinkling in my ears. I watched the clouds stretch out like cotton balls with the smallest of threads keeping them together in the middle of Sofie's "ba du bops" and "ba duba dops." I think her dad's singing lessons of not saying real words have really been paying off. I must have stayed there with my eyes half-open for nearly twenty minutes, sinking more and more into the ground until I almost fell asleep.

Just before the end of recess, Sofie gently tapped on my tennis shoes. I got up a little dizzy, and fixed my ponytail right away. It almost felt like we had just finished a long trip together. Sofie took a deep breath, and I looked down at what she made. The candy tracing made a shape of myself I had never seen before. My arms and legs were spread out almost like the X on a treasure map. Sofie did the tiniest of dances watching my smile grow.

I wish the two of us could have jumped into the wrappers like a real pile of leaves, but there wasn't enough time. We both knew that we would have to fill up the box and let things go back to normal again as soon as the bell rang. The candy thudded into the cardboard like a broken heartbeat. Have you ever been so happy and so sad at the same time? As we put the pieces back where they belonged, the cold wind came out of nowhere between the trees. Sofie sniffled her nose, and I started moving faster just to warm up.

Then out of the blue, Sofie asked me, "What does the name Ellie mean to you?" I didn't want to tell her it meant "beautiful" to somebody else, and I especially didn't want to tell her that I never wanted a girl name to begin with. I just looked away and said, "I don't know."

She put her hands on her hips and asked me, "So, what's your name?"

I was surprised she asked me that, but I surprised myself even more. The leaves danced in the new wind, and I zipped up my jacket. I told her, "My name is Rowan."

It's funny because I never actually thought of that name before. It just slipped out. Now that I think about it, that's probably how a lot of true things are said.

Sofie smiled and put the lid back onto the box. I wonder if she found this change beautiful too.

If she asked me "How are you?" right then, I would have said "I'm really, really good," and I would have been telling the absolute truth. Do you want to be asked about how you are right now? It's good to ask questions. Either way, I hope you like this balloon as much as I do, even if they are kind of bad for the Earth. This one is red and matches the tree in our front yard perfectly. It's nice to watch the colors fly up instead of fall down like always.

Anyways, thanks for listening. I hope you have a really good sleep.

Sincerely,
Rowan

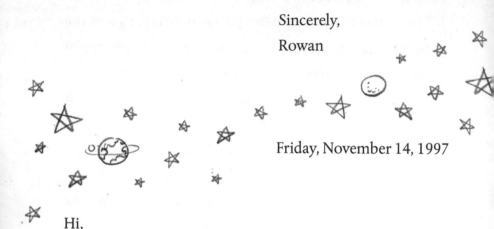

Friday, November 14, 1997

Hi,

I'm feeling so alone right now and haven't left my refrigerator box since my after-school snack. I thought Dylan Beaman was in an extra good mood today because he got a cool Koosh ball and a gun for his birthday. Plus, he brought those little ice cream cups with the wooden spoons for everyone in class. I just wish I had known it was his birthday sooner. I would have tried harder to make him happy again.

He looked at my long division quiz at the end of math class, then whispered in a loud way, "Why are you using a boy's name when you're a girl?" I didn't want to erase my name, but I also wanted Dylan Beaman to like me.

I've been secretly calling myself Rowan for the past week. I like how it feels, more than any name I've ever had. I've written it on nearly every assignment. Dylan Beaman must have figured it out because he likes to read off of my papers looking for answers. I thought that I was safe this whole entire time if I just avoided talking out loud. Dylan Beaman's question about being a real girl was as stressful as the parent-teacher conference plus winter concert rehearsals plus slumber parties times infinity plus ten. I squeezed my new basketball pencil until I thought I would snap it in half. Maybe Dylan wouldn't ever have a crush on me back if I'm not a girl.

That was the only time in my life I have ever wished for Dylan Beaman to stop staring at me. I wished Sofie or anybody else would have decided right then to use the noisy sharper next to our desks. I did the next best thing, and pretended not to hear Dylan ask about my name. I went through my pencil case for no reason. I pulled out some shavings, my new eraser, and reached back in for who knows what. The truth is I can't forget his question. "Why are you using a boy's name when you're a girl?" I might not ever forget it. The whole thing makes me afraid to write the name Rowan down ever again, but maybe it doesn't matter as long as I make all the other answers right for Dylan Beaman.

Thank goodness Mr. B finally came back from the bathroom and it was time for spelling. He put his hair into a little bun and started talking about how limited life would be if we only had five letters in the alphabet. I don't know. Maybe he said that to make us feel better about spelling, but how to spell things is something that I forget how to do no matter how many letters I have. I seem to always forget the words that are obvious to everybody else.

Dylan Beaman hardly listens to Mr. B, but he is still an impressive speller. Dylan even knows the bonus words that go at the very end of all the tests. He even knew how to spell out that miners' lung disease, pneumonoultramicroscopicsilicovolcanoconiosis, like it was no big deal. For Pete's sake, why does he think that the name Rowan is weird, but that word isn't? I had to look that up in the dictionary just to write it down in this letter.

Dylan Beaman didn't have a reason to look my way for the whole hour after that. He stayed glued to his own paper and we didn't even have the blue plastic dividers up. He knows that I am no good at spelling. It's actually the only subject he isn't a copycat for. I just wish that Dylan Beaman would find other ways to think of me as important and, yeah, I know letting someone cheat is really serious business. But I don't want to get him into big trouble, especially since his parents might use a belt. I don't want him to get hurt because of me. So I will never tell on him, or anybody else for that matter.

Believe it or not, the day got even harder after that. I saw cheetah print Lisa Frank invitations for Mary's party on some of my classmates' desks, and I'm not sure if I'm going to get one. My old friends haven't made fun of me in a while, but that's also because they haven't said anything to me at all. Maybe I should start wearing the shirt with my first initial *E* over the heart so they remember me better. Maybe Dylan will like that too.

I know that everybody might be busy hunting and playing euchre with their friends at deer camp with deer season starting, but I hope someone thinks to write me. I know I have Sofie for a friend now, but I just wish more people liked me. I used to ask whoever found my balloon mail to leave me a response under the WELCOME TO HOUGHTON sign next to Portage Bridge, but to be honest I haven't checked there in almost a month. I feel like I'm giving up on something, but I'm not sure on what exactly. Sorry.

Sincerely,
Ellie Beck

Thursday, November 27, 1997

Hello,

I'm trying my best today to be less sad about stuff because it's Thanksgiving and I heard that there's a balloon parade all the way in New York City that everyone wants to watch. The weird thing is some newspeople showed a map of the USA and completely forgot to color in where we live in Michigan's Upper Peninsula. The whole country was watching and they didn't include us. Don't other people know we are here? I don't know.

Anyways, I know I said I was feeling really alone in my last letter, I even skipped a week of writing, but I decided it's okay to be alone right now because then no one can tell me what my holiday tradition has to be. Ever since we moved to Houghton, my mom has had this Thanksgiving tradition of being on a not-so-secret diet and washing the dishes as loud as she can. My dad has a tradition of accidentally staying at deer camp with his old work friends for too long. It makes our house extra quiet with him gone. So, my mom and I keep it that way by eating chicken noodle soup and frozen pie in front of the TV. Sometimes it's so quiet sitting together, it feels like we're in trouble even if we're not. Please don't tell anybody that I said that. I don't know. Holidays are weird, but maybe they could be good someday.

Yesterday we actually had a half day at school, and we celebrated both Thanksgiving and a bunch of the boys in class coming back from deer camp. The cafeteria served special turkey lunches and had brown, orange, and yellow decorations, and everybody said, "What happens at deer camp stays at deer camp." Mr. B had his own plan for our class, of course. He turned off the *Reading Rainbow* special about Six Nations people, and gave us a long speech about how we should practice thankfulness every day and not just some days. Mr. B then said that our big job for that day was to make Thanksgiving cards, which is usually easy to do by turning our hands into turkeys. The bad news is that we had to use our old assignment that listed ten things we remember and ten things we love to inspire the insides of our cards.

I can't believe Mr. B held on to all of those giant pieces of paper. He pulled them out of the world's biggest manila folder and handed them out one by one. I had my fingers crossed that I would never have to look at that assignment again. I stared out into space for way too long because I knew that I didn't do it the way I was supposed to. My lists were a true incomplete, but Mr. B didn't say anything about it when he put it on my desk. He didn't even put any red marks on the paper. I thought for a minute about using my own red marker to do it for him.

Mr. B then said, "Feel free to move your desks together any way you want to while making your cards." The room cheered, but at that point I didn't even care. I sank into my chair. Dylan Beaman got up super fast and pulled his desk to other side of the classroom with a spiky-haired boy and my old friends. It was probably a dream come true for them. The girls all fixed their headbands when the boys came over, and

I sank even lower as Mr. B gave different groups small buckets of art supplies.

I decided in that moment that it was probably best that no one sat near me, not even Sofie. She seemed like she was too busy following the teacher's directions to notice me anyways. I hoped for a minute it would stay that way. I listed her name in my "Ten things I love" list, and what if seeing that on my page makes her feel weird? Even worse, what if someone in class ends up seeing it? Love is even worse than calling someone cute. Just to be safe, I folded the old assignment in half and watched one of the orange markers slowly roll off my desk. It plopped on the ground and rolled farther and farther away. Not even the markers wanted to sit with me. I didn't care about that either, though. Space was better. The room got louder. Dylan Beaman's laugh did too. I wasn't so sure what to feel thankful about.

Eventually, Sofie pulled her desk over. I folded the old assignment into another half just in case she could see the words through the paper. I felt her eyes on me, but I didn't want anyone else in the room to think that I was glad that Sofie was there or that I have been to her house. I put my head down on the table and let my hair stretch all the way across the surface. She slowly slid over a big piece of paper and asked, "Can I use your hand for my Thanksgiving card?"

Sofie picked up the orange marker that fell onto the ground and scooted herself over until there was no space between us. Have you ever said that you want something, and maybe you meant the complete opposite? All I'm saying is, maybe I didn't want to sit alone in class after all.

I finally sat up, and she pressed my hand into the page. I felt my whole palm get bigger under hers. Sofie gently moved the marker in between my fingers spread across the paper. When she finally let go, she said "Ta-dah." Then she started coloring it in, ignoring the teacher's directions completely. She didn't even bother turning the tracing into a turkey. Maybe she was thankful enough to have the shape of my hand to keep for later.

But then giggles came from the other side of the room. They weren't the nice kind. Courtney and Mary fake held hands to match us. My cheeks turned a whole new kind of pink. Maybe it was bad that I liked holding Sofie's hand. I just wish the power had gone out or that quiet boy, Nathan Lucas, had suddenly done something really loud and distracting. I wish they all just forgot about me again. Sometimes even a half day of school is way too long.

Then, after another wave of big laughing, my old BFFs all started singing Spice Girls songs. Gina has the best voice, but was singing the least. She watched me and Sofie with big eyes until Dylan Beaman suddenly flicked his new school store eraser. He wanted to get them to stop singing that song, "Stop right now thank you very much." Maybe he doesn't like it when anyone sings. This is probably weird, but I kind of wanted him to flick his eraser at me too. I don't know why. All I can say is thank goodness my old friends didn't sing that "Sitting in a tree k-i-s-s-i-n-g" song about me and Sofie. I would have fainted.

Those girls used to be Sofie's friends too, but they decided she was too different a long time ago, even before that stupid slumber party last summer. I guess that's something Sofie and I have in common. Pretty please keep this between us, but I think it would be cool if one day Sofie and I were grown-ups together in a different city and did things we would never do at our bathroom meetings. Maybe I could watch her do that "I've given you everything, all that joy can bring, yes I swear" song at a karaoke place with lots of lights and Shirley Temples.

Sofie touched my shoulder then said, "Can I trace your other hand too? So this one could have a friend?"

I tried to hide my smile and closed my eyes. I gave Sofie my second hand to outline onto the same page. When she finished, she looked at the paper and gave it a big hug. Have you ever given a piece of paper a hug? I do it sometimes, but not usually in front of other people. The Thanksgiving card came out so nice. I felt lucky to know a part of me gets to go home with her. Maybe she will even use it as a placemat at her family's Thanksgiving dinner. Sofie told me that Richard is going to make sweet potatoes with marshmallows on top. I think he's a genius. They'll also have special cranberry sauce and greens. I hope they had fun together and they liked everything they ate. I hope you had a good dinner too, and that you find ways to be thankful every day like Mr. B says, even though it's really hard sometimes.

I'm thankful that I had a good dream last night. It was about melting icicles and absolutely everything was blue, not just the sky. Sofie was in my dream for the very first time too. She was wearing a white dress and I used one of the icicles from her porch to heal her scraped knees. The water dripped down her leg and formed a river big enough for us to swim in. I'm thankful that happened even though it didn't actually happen in real life.

I woke up thinking about who I would want to sit with me when I have my own Thanksgiving one day. Maybe there won't be a lot of people there, and that's fine, I think. I would still make sure that everyone arrives to the dinner party in Selena carriages, and we would all share marshmallows and a long table with a paper tablecloth to keep tracing each other's hands. Maybe we could use the tablecloth to make the world's biggest paper sailboat, or hat if you flip it the other way.

Maybe it sounds all silly to you because you don't know anyone else with those traditions, but you can be part of them if you want to, whoever you are. You don't have to decide right now, though. It's going to be a while until I become a grown-up and can have my own house to do things like that. I can't even buy a bag of marshmallows with my one-dollar allowance, let alone a table big enough for everyone to fit around for our big meal. Actually, while writing this letter, I ate some reheated chicken noodle soup. So it's kind of like you and I had a meal together just now. I am thankful for that too. But I'm sorry about spilling some Vernor's on the paper. We can just pretend it's the tablecloth we shared.

Thank you for reading about my life,
Rowan

Sunday, November 30, 1997

Dear Whoever You Are,

The whole world seemed to be frozen this weekend. And I'm not talking about the Turkey Bowl Skate at the ice rink or all those plows everyone is attaching to their pickup trucks. I won my own no talking game with two whole days straight without saying a word out loud. With Dad still out of town, Mom has been doing a pretty good job at the game too. Maybe this was cheating, but I used my finger to write the word "hi" and lots of hearts into the frost on my bedroom window. All I could really see on the other side of the glass was the gray house next door and Jax's mom brushing her long hair in that cozy-looking yellow bedroom.

If you ever get to read this, know that it must have taken a real miracle for it to get to you. There must be a billion-trillion snowflakes outside. It's hard to believe that anything can fly when there is so much falling on top of it. Everybody says that the cold and copper are what make us strong. It's good to be strong, but I don't know.

I guess there are some things I like about the cold weather. I love ice-skating, especially when I get to do it under the sky. The cold also reminds me of parts of myself I usually forget about, like my toes, my chin, and especially my ears. They tingle and can't be ignored on days like these. Yesterday, I remembered my breath too. It showed up right in front of me while I was walking down the driveway. I took a breath, and I was suddenly surrounded by my own clouds. It was like I was the only person in the world.

I eventually got to the mailbox, but there were no letters or birthday invitations inside. There was only a magazine for Mom. The front cover bragged about George Clooney being the best person in the world. I wonder what it's like for the whole country to think that you're beautiful. The mailbox lid made a sad rusty sound when I closed it with George still inside. I betcha Mom will be happy to see him when she gets home from work.

I pulled down the red flag and walked back to our little

white house, where nothing ever seems to change. All the lights were off and the driveway was still empty, and I felt big and lonely with every step that crunched into the snow. There weren't even raccoons rattling the trash can or birds in the birdhouse. Do you happen to know why birds fly south? I wonder if they ever fly back to certain places because they feel like they have to.

I went back inside the house, up the stairs, and into my room with empty hands. I'm not even sure why getting mail would make much of a difference. The truth is, weekends often feel frozen to me. It feels like forever to see who I want to see again. I get people-sick, not homesick.

Even though Dylan Beaman and I also don't talk much, I was missing him too. It's just nice always having somebody to sit next to. When I was at church today, I couldn't stop thinking about getting back to school and having the chance to have our desks so close to each other again. The priest just said his usual things, so instead I watched the snow fall outside thinking about what Dylan might have been doing in that moment. I wonder what he does when he's all alone. I wonder how tight he holds his covers, or if he has ever gone outside to wish on snowflakes like falling stars. I wonder if he likes deer better alive or hanging on a wall. Who are you usually thinking about when the world gets all quiet? How do you know if they are thinking about you too? I don't know.

Later, when I got home from today's Mass, I ran up to my

room and cleared all the frost off with my sleeve to see if my dog was outside. He wasn't, but the "Shake, Shake, Shake" song that Sofie wrote got stuck in my head all of a sudden. I guess Sofie was stuck in my head too. This is just between us, but I've been missing Sofie too. I couldn't go to her house, though, because Thanksgiving weekend is only supposed to be for family time, and I had to be home to greet Dad back from deer camp. It's whatever, though. I just had to give him a hug and he fell asleep on the couch real fast, but like I said, it's whatever.

Things right now are good in my room and out the window too. I'll just keep on humming Sofie's song, and the snowflakes are extra beautiful sparkling under the streetlights. Snowflakes that glow with a little help are my favorite kind. These ones are so round that I bet there is a whole world on top of each of them. Wait, I have an idea. I'll be right back.

Okay, I'm back now. Thanks for waiting. In case you were wondering, I went downstairs, put on my mittens, and walked right by sleeping Dad and tired Mom. Don't worry, though. They were facing the TV for their favorite cop show, I think it's just called *Cops*. I managed to find an empty grape jelly jar behind the piles of fresh venison in the fridge. I brought the jar outside, and quietly closed the front door behind me.

As I stepped under the streetlight, everything was a shade of yellow. A truck with a dusty top drove by. The snowflakes jumped and included me in their flurry dance. So many of them kissed me on the face and even though they were made of ice, they warmed my cheeks. Maybe this is what heaven would be like if there is one. To keep the feeling closer, I opened the glass jar and held it into the air.

Snowflakes flew into the container like wintertime fireflies. They kept moving even with the lid closed. It is a real snow globe, the realest one that I've ever had. Before I went back inside, I gave the jar a hug. I'm going to give it to Sofie before school starts tomorrow.

I hope you got to go outside today too.

Sincerely,
Rowan Beck

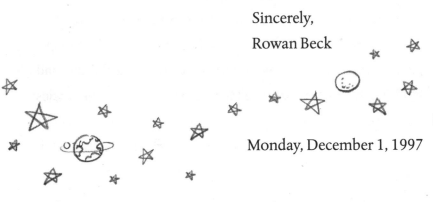

Monday, December 1, 1997

Hello Out There,

I know I would get in big trouble for saying this, but I wish I could trade my dad for Sofie's. I'm not really sure what to do about that. I really wish something could change. I wish I could do something to help. Sorry, I'm sorry. I'll explain.

First you should know that all of the flakes in my homemade snow globe melted by the time I got to school this morning. It became a jar full of dirty-looking water. I know it's basic science, but for a second I thought it was all my fault that the snow went away. I wasn't so sure if it was still a good gift, but I decided to give it to Sofie anyways. She was extra quiet, quieter than the snow, when I saw her by the flagpole before school. At first, I thought she was just mad that we didn't have a snow day or she got grounded or something. I whispered "Hi," and gave her the jar. We looked at each other through the curved glass. Her eyes were full of water, and they stayed that way all morning long. She even left spelling this morning to have a bathroom meeting all by herself.

Later that day at recess, I decided to give her my striped wool mittens because she forgot hers. The fourth graders nearby were busy screaming and rolling up the biggest snowball in history, but Sofie didn't look over at them once. She spoke in a voice I could hardly recognize. "Papa was in the wrong place at the wrong time, and now he's gone for who knows how long."

The truth is her dad, Richard, had to go to jail last minute. It's like he went to a whole other world too, and not the good kind. Sofie's eyes and shoulders melted the more that she talked about it. It turns out that Richard was just buying marshmallows for their sweet potato tradition, but there was accidentally leftover tape covering his car lights from when we all painted together. He got pulled over, and arrested, and fought when he shouldn't have. Sofie cried, "Don't you know, it's illegal to say no to people in charge. It's illegal to have no light even if your car looks like a white carriage. It's all my fault." Sofie laid her head on my lap. It was the first time I didn't care about people staring at us at recess.

Have you ever had a friend melt before? Did you know the right thing to say? All I could say was "It's not your fault, I promise." She nodded and turned her face to the gray side of our giant rock, the snow globe still in her hands. She twirled the dirty water into a small winter storm and held it close, waiting for it to get crystals again. Nothing changed. She then brought the jar to her chest and shook it again. Again, nothing.

She shivered with feelings and curled into my belly button. I'm not sure if that's the safest place in the world, but I leaned forward over her body to be a blanket for her. I could barely feel Sofie between the thick of our winter coats, but I knew she must have been in there somewhere with her teeth chattering. In that moment, over Sofie's curls, I noticed a logging truck bounce down the street. I pressed into her back a little extra hoping that she wouldn't see it drive by. Richard wouldn't be working his job again until he gets enough money to get out of jail. I'm not sure how that even works when it's not playing Monopoly.

But I think Sofie saw the logging truck disappear down

Military Road anyways. She sat up all of a sudden and told me, "I think I just want to be alone right now." Her eyes were big and sure with their own crystals inside. I hugged her cushioned back one more time, and left her there in the icy dead grass.

I waited on top of the big play structure, my feet dangled off the wooden sides, ready to come back down whenever she needed me. From below the fake bridge, I could hear my old friends talking away. Mary told the group that she wanted a cheetah-print snap bracelet and a game called Dream Phone for her birthday. Mary then said, "You're all going to be at the party, right?" I know that she wasn't talking to me, and I almost didn't even care. My ears felt so much wind from the top of the structure that I could feel them changing colors. To keep a little warmer, I hid my hands in my pockets, deep enough to feel the lint and the little hole I've been trying to ignore.

I watched Sofie keep her face pressed to the snow globe for the whole rest of recess. I hope having something to hold made her feel less alone. Next time maybe I will get her an icicle like in that dream I had the other day. I would even be willing to ice-skate across Lake Superior to find the very best one. Sofie makes me wonder a lot. She also makes me want to give, and go outside even when everything feels frozen and I have to remember my ears and hands again.

I just really, super hope that somebody finds this balloon

letter because I have a big, huge favor to ask you. When you have the chance, could you please send Sofie Gavia a nice note or something good to William Henderson Elementary on Military Road in Houghton, Michigan? You can let her know that she deserves the very best world. Sometimes it is helpful to hear things like that from a stranger because then it almost feels like it's a message from God. I don't know, I just want her to feel like it's possible to be at the right place at the right time again.

Thanks,
Rowan

P.S. Even though I usually stay in the bathroom during church, please know that I have been really, really good lately. I've been doing my chores every week, and I have no incomplete homework at school. I still think nice things about my old friends even when they probably don't think nice things about me. I would just really like it if you did me this favor, and sent a letter or something nice to Sofie. She gave me a rock on my front porch today even if probably she didn't mean to say "I'm okay."

Thanks again,
Rowan

Dear Whoever Is Listening,

I put my hamper in front of my bedroom door. Don't ask why. I'm doing my best to remember what better times in life were like. By the way, does your dad live with you? Are you glad about it? I don't know. I know that I should just be grateful for having a dad after what happened to Sofie, but I don't know. Even though winter just started, it sure is hard to remember what it's like on the other side of it.

Lately, it has been helping me to make maps to my favorite places. That way, I will never forget how to get there once everything is covered with snow. Sometimes when my favorite places seem super-duper far away, I pretend it is inside of my body. That way, I can go whenever I want. Do you think something is pretending if it feels real? I'm not sure. When Dad left my room the other day, I just closed my eyes and retraced my steps to my favorite river. It felt like spring again.

Today Sofie and I walked way, way out of the way to get home after school just so we could walk along that same river. We actually decided to leave school together when the bell rang instead of hiding in the stalls for everyone else to leave first like usual. I didn't want to waste time worrying about my old friends' thoughts about us. Even though Sofie told me the other day that she didn't want to talk about her dad anymore, I could tell that she was still having a hard time about it. She kept her eyes down and felt so far away even though we were right next to each other. I tucked my hair into my hat, and we both kept quiet for the first fifteen minutes of our walk to Pilgrim River. There were no clouds in the sky, but it kept on snowing. The forest felt endless with our big crunchy steps.

Then, out of the blue, the two of us saw mysterious dog prints in the snow and I said, "Let's follow them." Sofie's face unthawed. We named the dog Balto even though we never actually got to meet him. It was nearly impossible to see the paw prints after a few minutes of walking because everything was the brightest white. The tree branches hung low and heavy with ice along the blanketed river. It felt like everything was getting erased. We eventually got to a point where the snowmobile trail ended and there were no more dog tracks to be found. Our legs started to get lost in the deep snow like quicksand, and it was scary because my shoes weren't made for this season.

Luckily, there were some other human footprints left for us ahead. They were big, probably from grown-ups, and so Sofie and I came up with a new game without hardly saying anything at all. We had to fit all four of our feet into one shoeprint. It only lasted one round because we both knew right away that we wouldn't ever fit into what was left behind. We had to step outside of those footprints if we really wanted to walk side by side, and so we did. The snow went all the way to our knees.

I bit my lip trying to be strong about the cold like everybody else who lives here. Some of the ice got inside of my shoes, but I promised myself not to say anything about it. I didn't want to bring Sofie down after we survived all that. Either way, that snow melted in no time and filled the spaces in between my toes. It felt miserable, but it was a good reminder that the river water doesn't actually disappear. If anything, we were surrounded by more water than ever. My favorite place wasn't gone, it only changed shape. I let the cold spread and stayed brave by humming some winter concert music and then that *Sound of Music* song about raindrops on kittens and roses on mittens. I actually surprised myself since I haven't used my voice like that since Halloween.

After who knows how long, we stopped in our tracks, so Sofie could put on those mittens I gave her. She wiggled her fingers in until they fit her perfectly. The snow started falling again, and a few snowflakes landed on her eyelashes, like they wanted to listen to what came next. She told me in an almost-whisper, "I have a brand-new favorite place. It's the space between the Christmas tree and the living room wall. Me and Papa picked the tree out together."

I know she said she didn't want to talk about her dad,

but it was her first real smile of the day. It didn't last long, though. Sofie's eyes started to water the more she talked about their real pine tree. Richard's logging job meant they know how to pick the best one in the whole entire forest. Now Mrs. Gavia brings Sofie's dinner plate behind the tree, just she can stay close to the place she loves. I think that's nice of her mom.

I looked at Sofie again, and she had at least ten more snowflakes on her eyelashes. She looked up and said a little louder than before, "Things will go back to normal soon." I hope she is right.

In the meantime, I really want to learn everything I can about her new favorite place behind her tree. My Christmas tree at home is made of plastic and has bulbs that all came perfectly matching from the same box. It feels too perfect and probably hasn't seen any snow. I don't think it grew out of any place at all. I wonder about all the snowflakes that fell onto Sofie's Christmas tree when it still lived in the forest and how long they stayed on once the Gavias took it home. I wonder if the snowflakes missed each other when it was time to go. Probably not too much because one day they will melt into the same river and evaporate into the same sky. I don't know.

Sofie then said to me, "It's getting late. I need to get home to babysit Viivi." I really wanted more time walking between the pine trees together, but instead I waved goodbye to Sofie. She sighed and walked away. I listened to her crunch get smaller and smaller until the sound was gone.

I've been thinking about asking Sofie if she wants to come over to my house. Maybe we could use my basement refrigerator box to go sailing without a map, travel to the moon, or go anywhere she wants to, a place where nothing bad could ever happen. I was going to ask her that at the end of our walk, but I didn't know how. Fifth graders aren't supposed to play like that.

I looked back behind me one more time half believing I would see her standing there, but she was gone. Only our footsteps were still there, side by side.

I know we haven't met before, you and me, but can I be honest with you about something? Sometimes I'm afraid the places I want to go to aren't really worth thinking about. Sometimes it's just not as easy as making a map. I want to share more, but I first want someone to promise me that they will love me no matter what. At church they say that's what God is for, but I don't know.

I have to go now. I hope you find your favorite place.

Sincerely,
Rowan

Dear (put your name here),

We did my favorite tradition of putting up Christmas lights in the front yard today. I think my nose hair froze up, but the lights came out really cool. Dad bought a new beer brand to celebrate. He actually said, "I want to make sure the new kind tastes good," and walked off to take a hydration break within the first few minutes of decorating. I didn't mind that he left because he usually gets mad if the lights don't go exactly how he wants. Anyways, Mom and I worked alone and had a good laugh while getting the lights just right on the bushes on the first try.

After that, my parents left for some kind of church thing where the marines give toys to somebody else's kids. Christmas is coming up, and so everyone is trying to be good about talking to God more. Dad would like an orange drill or a good working chain saw, Mom would like another magazine subscription. I haven't actually asked for this, but I would like a new haircut for Christmas. I would also really like a hot-air balloon, so I could find you instead of having to write these letters with regular balloons. A computer could be cool too, but they cost so much money and prob-

ably wouldn't even have Oregon Trail or that aliens geom-
etry game like the computers at school. Really, though, I just
want a haircut.

I do wonder whether or not Mary got the Dream Phone
game like she really wanted. I wouldn't know. Her big party
was last night and my invitation officially never came. After
having fun at McDonald's, they probably had Bagel Bites and
watched a PG-13 movie even though she's turning eleven.
It's okay I wasn't there, I guess. I'm just thankful that they
didn't try to prank-call me or anything like that. Have you
ever seen a PG-13 movie before? It's okay if you haven't. Me
neither, except for the last slumber party, where we watched
*Austin Powers* and then turned off the lights to listen to that
scary story about the girl with the ribbon around her neck.

Anyways, whatever. It's okay. Tonight was good. As soon
as I heard my parents leave for the church thing, I hopped
out of my bed. I ate my last piece of Halloween candy and
looked for my dog out the window. Jax wasn't there. Instead
of staying alone all night long, I decided to invite Sofie over
using our brand-new secret signal. Please be cool and don't
tell anyone else what it is because it really is a secret.

All I had to do is walk ten minutes to Sofie's house, and
put a special red rock on her front porch. I just had to put
it there by eight o'clock, so she didn't accidentally fall asleep
first. I found the rock in front of this house where there is
no garden, but they have a flag for every holiday. Some-

times I find ones just like it in big piles around Houghton, and if you dig deep enough you can even find some copper. Tonight's rock looked like it came from outer space and had little specks of silver trapped inside. It shined when I placed it under Sofie's porch light.

Nothing happened right away, so secretly I peeked between their plastic blinds. The TV was playing some show about winning an island if people know how to spell the right words. I would be so bad at that game. No one was there watching it, but I knew deep down that Sofie would see our secret signal after tucking in her baby sister. I skipped back home through the dusty snow, and couldn't help but look at the neon-blue sky. The moon was out so big and bright, like it was trying to climb over gravity to kiss me good-night.

And guess what. Sofie got to my house only a few minutes after me. She knocked three times for the secret password, and smiled with six teeth showing when I opened the front door. She walked in fast, handed me her Selena tape, and the two of us got straight to work on preparing our refrigerator box. You might think it's all baby-talk make-believe, but it was actually a lot of fun thinking about sailing our box boat up to the moon.

Sofie giggled and said, "Okay, we are going to need a ladder or hot-air balloon, and so many picnic baskets to keep full for the long journey. We need to be prepared for anything." She then talked about us needing special straws to breathe out of if we're traveling to outer space. I almost couldn't tell if she was serious or not. I looked behind my shoulder, not even sure how all of that stuff was going to fit into the sunflower suitcase I already started packing that morning. I unzipped my bag again and decided not to bring my lava lamp to make room for what we would really need. I wrapped the cord around the lamp's body, and asked Sofie, "Do you want any Swiss Miss? We have extra marshmallows."

She nodded her head, but then she looked sad all of a sudden. Sofie asked, "Rowan, there aren't any jails on the moon, right?" Just so you know, there aren't. There is also no gravity to pull people down.

I promised her with all of my heart, "In space, there are only sky and rocks, and maybe even an ice rink inside the craters. There are only things that we love."

She nodded again, this time with her dimples showing. I felt kind of bad about reminding Sofie of her dad by mentioning marshmallows, but we went into the kitchen anyways. Together we took turns stirring the Swiss Miss into the milk with a little plastic spoon. I put them in the microwave, pressed Start, and asked , "Do you still want to go to the moon?" She jumped up with a "Yes" as if we were only inches away from it.

The microwave buzzed and we finished packing in the living room. I found my Pokémon cards binder and ice skates. Sofie pulled a ladder in from the garage. We added them to the pile that seemed to grow and grow around our refrigerator box. Sofie looked so happy when she wiped her hands clean and said, "I think the microwave is beeping. I'll be right back with our hot chocolates."

Do you ever get really sad, and it just comes out of nowhere? I hate to admit this, but that's what happened to me as soon as Sofie went back to the kitchen. I looked at our pile of supplies and only saw a mess. I wanted so badly to make our adventure feel real again, but I wrapped my arms around my legs and held my eyes like they needed handholds. The moon seemed farther and farther away the more that we tried to get there. Do you know what I mean? I almost wanted to give up completely. I imagined all of the kids at school knowing what we were up to, and saying that it's stupid. I wouldn't know how to tell them that they're wrong.

I didn't even know that anybody was listening when I blabbed, "We're never going to be able to make a map big enough to get to the moon. We're gonna be stuck in this place forever and ever and ever and ever." But when I peeked between my fingers, I was surprised to see Sofie standing there smiling with twelve teeth. Each hot chocolate sitting on the windowsill was filled to the top with marshmallows.

Right away, Sofie took my Michigan-shaped hands and led me to the living room window.

But it was too late and too dark to see hardly anything outside, even the moon was covered up. The glass only bounced back our own reflections, and Sofie's curls looked like a wonderful cloud. She pointed toward the glass and said, "If you want to get to the moon, we can just follow the constellation of freckles on your arm." I looked in my window reflection trying to see what she could see.

I didn't believe it at first, but Sofie was right. My left arm alone has at least fifteen little brown freckles. I had never thought about my body having its very own starry map. I traced them one by one with my finger until the moon reappeared. It was so good to see it out the window again, but I couldn't help suddenly feeling full of more bad questions about the future, about the other kids at school. About Sofie's dad never coming back, about my dad never going away. I said to Sofie, "Do you think people will be nice to us on the moon?"

Sofie had a lightbulb moment all of a sudden. She ran into my basement and I listened to her feet thud all the way down the stairs. Sofie came back just two minutes later.

She came back carrying a strand of Christmas lights, the same kind we used to decorate our house. Without a word, she wrapped the strand around my shoulders, through my ponytail, all the way past my line of freckles, and back down to the ground. I lit up in every direction, even before she plugged the white lights in. She finally responded to my question. She said, "You are a star." That made me smile with a lot of teeth. It almost felt like there were more teeth in my smile than there were stars in the sky.

I said, "You are too."

Every once in a while, I go to sleep thinking how lucky am I to have a story like this to tell someone. If I had gone to Mary's silly slumber party, I probably would have been too afraid to tell my old friends anything at all. I would have only done dares and eaten potato chips. Maybe I would have ended up in another one of their home videos.

Instead, right before Sofie left tonight, I gave her my Rapunzel Barbie so she could have some help babysitting Viivi. She placed the doll on her shoulder and told me, "Good night, Rowan." No one has ever said that to me before.

For the record, my parents still don't know that Rowan exists. They don't even know Rowan's laugh or what Rowan thinks about. One day, I'd like to be Rowan at church and at the dinner table because he is my favorite version of myself. Is it okay that I said *he* right there? I don't know. I hope so. Either way, thanks for not thinking I'm too weird to listen to.

Good night,
Rowan Beck

Hi,

You know how everybody gets a birthday wish? Does everyone get a Christmas wish too? I guess I'm just wondering exactly how many wishes do I get every year and if there's anything I could do to get more.

For the last month, Dylan Beaman's most favorite place in the world has been the paper football field. The championships have been taking place at our desks nearly every day before school starts, and that's major news. Pretty much every boy in class is there. I have to admit, though, it's kind of like the burping contests. I can only watch from the sidelines, otherwise they think I'm in the way. Nobody has told me that with their words, but trust me, I know a stink eye when I see one.

It's really great to see Dylan Beaman happy doing his thing, though. When the boys do the big paper football flick, they all get quiet and then scream. Dylan jumps up and nods his head a bunch. It's maybe no secret to you reading this, but I think I have a crush on him. I've never told him, and now would actually be the worst time ever for him to know. Word travels fast around here, especially when everybody and their brother now knows how to fold cootie catchers. I just like watching Dylan Beaman, whether or not he knows I'm there.

Before class even started, he smiled at me and had a twinkle in his eyes. I almost thought he was showing off just for me. He really knew that I was there, and actually looked happy about it. He flicked his paper football so perfectly afterward that it flew right in between his friend's hands on the other side of the field. Dylan scored big for his Green Bay team, and I like to think that I somehow helped him get that point. But the truth is that he is at his nicest when he is already winning.

There were high fives and "boo-yahs" left and right. Dylan Beaman stood tall out of his chair to celebrate. I clapped maybe too loud, but I felt lucky to know that the biggest game of the season happened thanks to our desks getting pushed together. I decided right then and there to make Dylan Beaman paper footballs for his Christmas present. I kept my smile for the rest of the school day thinking about all the good things that this could lead to. Even Mr. B noticed. He walked by my desk while I was reading a new *Goosebumps* at SRT. He said to me, "It looks like you've been coloring with new crayons," making me blush even more than before.

Then at recess, while all the other kids were playing king of the mountain on their snow forts, I sat under the jungle gym and taught myself how to fold my very own paper footballs. I think you would have been proud of me because some things are really hard to make without directions. Sofie sat by my side drawing pictures of cats to mail her dad. She was having a quiet day since our winter concert rehearsal this morning and didn't say a word about all the pages I tore out of my notebook. It took me nearly seventy pieces of paper to make the same triangle shape that all the other boys have mastered. Three or four of the footballs I folded at recess maybe passed as almost perfect. The edges weren't smooth, but they were at least symmetrical and had nice colors. I put them in my pocket, careful not to show them to anyone too soon.

But when the last bell of the day rang, I was ready. I even daydreamed about showing Dylan this cool new thing we have in common. After that, the two of us would walk out of the school's front doors together and into the afternoon sunset. Doesn't walking next to anyone feel like a big deal to you? It's different from standing or sitting next to somebody. Walking together means that you're going to the same place and I just wanted to go to the same place as Dylan Beaman, or at least pretend until it was time for us to go to our own houses.

I stood at my hallway cubby locker, and got ready to go in super slow motion until Dylan stepped out of the classroom. He hardly noticed me at first. I pulled on the rest of my coat real casual, put on my blue hat, and tucked in my hair ready to go. But when he walked by, all I could do was blurt out, "Bye, Dylan."

He looked at me from the side and softly said back, "Bye, Rowan." I was shocked because no one but Sofie has ever called me that name. Hearing Dylan Beaman say "Rowan" all sincere felt like a Christmas Miracle. I smiled toward the sky as if there were no ceiling at all. I quickly waved him over until his shadow showed up next to mine. I took the paper footballs out of my backpack one by one, three brown triangles and one blue and gray. I didn't know why his eyes were glued to the door at the end of the hallway instead.

I swear on my life, the paper footballs were folded almost perfectly. I held them closer to him in case he somehow couldn't see I had his favorite thing right in my hands. He blinked a few times, and whispered.

I almost don't even want to tell you what he said. He said, "I made a pact with the Trampoline Club and I can't talk to you anymore." My old friends made a name without me. I can't really say how this felt, so I will draw you a storm instead.

Dylan zipped up his puffy coat and walked away so fast. I heard what he said, but I didn't think he was going to stop talking to me right that very second. I really wanted to shout at him, "I know you are, but what am I?" or kick a wall. Do you think that it was it my fault somehow? I wonder if my old friends came up with this plan at that dang slumber party I was never invited to. I hope they didn't watch videos from Courtney's camcorder and turn me into a party game again. I just wish I could have done something to change Dylan's mind, but I guess a pact is a pact.

The big gray doors to the parking lot slammed behind Dylan, and he was gone. The hallway was so empty without him in it. It was just me, the janitor, and all of the school binders that my classmates left behind. I didn't think that it was possible to feel any more alone.

I decided to stay by my cubby locker for an extra while just so Dylan Beaman and I wouldn't accidentally see each other in the parking lot. I didn't want to make him feel weird. Still, I caught myself hoping and praying for him to come back through those doors just to say "... NOT" and hang out with me a little bit longer. He would have a whole apology dance ready just like Cory did for Topanga in the last episode of *Boy Meets World*. I don't know.

Honestly, all I really wanted was for him to use a football I made him for the next big game. I felt so silly still holding all of those paper triangles after he walked away. Everybody knows I just stand to the side during the games. A part of me really just wanted to crumple them all up, but I had to remember that I made them for myself too. I put them inside of my front backpack pocket, the one that I always forget about. That way, the paper footballs wouldn't get crushed by my school binder or anything else I carry around. Some things just feel impossible to keep safe.

Sorry, I just can't believe that the Trampoline Club got to Dylan so easy. One time, even when we were all still real friends, we played hide-and-seek at Mary's house and they all gave up on looking for me and went on to eat Fruit by the Foot snacks instead. I stayed under that green chair with the cat toys waiting for my friends to remember me for who knows how long. Hasn't anyone important ever forgotten about you? I can't be the only one, right? I just hope that their club doesn't get any bigger, or soon I will be the only person in the school who isn't in it.

I guess I can't blame Dylan for doing what they told him. I know how bad it feels to get in trouble.

You know, I think I'm going to start wearing my plastic headband again so my old friends can remember me better. I didn't officially put this on my Christmas list, but a real Christmas Miracle would be getting invited to a slumber party again. A real miracle would be Dylan Beaman forever remembering me as Rowan Beck. Since those things probably won't happen, I'm trying to be brave by remembering the things I like, lightning bolts and potato chips and burping, without Dylan or anybody's help. But the winter concert is just days away, and the thought of Dylan seeing me sing and wrinkling his nose again really scares me.

I'll shut up now.

Hope you're okay.<br>
Rowan

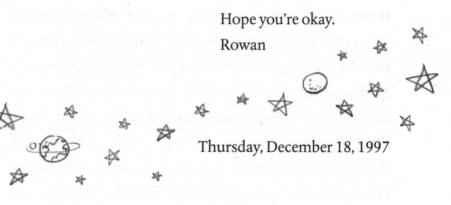

Thursday, December 18, 1997

Hi.

The dang winter concert is tomorrow. I don't know why it has to be this big tradition for us to sing songs that everybody has already heard a hundred million times. Doesn't the school know that not everybody's parents can be there? Sofie just drew pictures of white horses all recess long. She's getting really good at drawing and I wish that carriage could come alive for her, so she could have the concert her dad planned all along.

Honestly, the only good thing about the whole show is

that we got to skip SRT and language arts to rehearse this afternoon. Mr. B led all of the fourth and fifth graders to the gym. Then he and the music teacher made us get into four giant rows with tallest kids in the back and shortest in the front. The two teachers put their hands inside of their pockets and watched us all shuffle around the room like we have never done it before. A lot of the girls linked arms so they wouldn't have to break up. I was just trying to mind my own business and stay as far away from Dylan as possible. But I looked behind me and saw Sofie make her way to the back row with her hands gripping the horse drawings in her pockets. A paper airplane flew over her head, but I don't even think she noticed it.

The music teacher then put a peace sign in the air so everybody else would quiet down. We all raised our arms to match him while Mr. B gave us a big pep talk. He said something about singing with our whole voices, from our way deep insides and not just our throats. He said, "This is good practice in telling the truth." Maybe he was right, I don't know. Do you ever lie? I think I probably lie more to myself than to anybody. For example, I actually love to sing, but I've been telling myself that I don't like it ever since Halloween. I also tell myself that I like some of the outfits that Mom gives to me, even though I don't like them at all. Other times, I think I lie about sleeping when Dad visits my room. Sorry, maybe I shouldn't have said that. I guess what I'm trying to say is that sometimes it's easier to just go along with things.

The truth is that I can tell a lie without even talking, and I was for sure lying about my height when standing with all of the short kids at rehearsal today. Like I said, I just wanted to avoid standing next to Dylan Beaman at all costs. I hunched my shoulders and bent my knees to make myself smaller. I even took my shoes off to be a half an inch shorter knowing that the Trampoline Club was probably watching. The music teacher, of course, caught me. He tapped on my shoulder and asked me to go in the tall-kid back row right next to Dylan. I turned around toward the sea of fourth and fifth graders, now all staring straight ahead toward the boom box and empty folding chairs. I right away noticed Sofie with her hands covering her eyes right in the middle of it all. I wonder where she was.

Mr. B cleared this throat until I moved. He then reminded the whole room for the second time that day, "Don't stand in each other's light." I hope you know, I didn't mean to cover somebody's light by being in the front row. I still feel kind of sorry about it. How is it that making myself smaller still ended up being kind of selfish? It's confusing. Anyways, I went to the back, like the teachers told me to.

I know I should have cared more about not bothering Dylan, but I tried to lean a little forward to see if Sofie had opened her eyes yet. I wanted to see if she was okay. I was hoping and praying that nobody else would notice me, but my arm accidentally touched Dylan Beaman's striped sweater. He didn't move an inch. He was keeping his pact with the Trampoline Club.

Mr. B then turned on the little black stereo and shouted to us, "EXPAND!" I tried expanding by standing straight up to check on Sofie over Dylan's head. It actually wasn't until that very moment I realized that Dylan Beaman and I are the exact same height. I always thought I was at least a few inches shorter than him. Dylan looked back at me, and I swear for a moment he smiled in a nice way. I know that we aren't allowed to talk to each other ever again, or maybe not until the end of high school, but I wanted to give Dylan Beaman a compliment so he would like me again. I don't know. Instead, I just kept quiet for him.

After that, I really was doing my best to just move my lips while everybody else sang the fun version of "Rudolph." I know that using my little singing voice is not what Mr. B said to do. Here's the thing, though, I usually only use my whole voice when I am afraid, like when I scream on a roller coaster or when the soccer ball hits me funny in gym class. Whenever that happens, I always make myself promise to never do that thing again, so that nobody notices me. So, if I sing with my whole voice, I break a promise to myself. If I don't sing with my whole voice, I break a promise to the teacher. I break a promise no matter what, so I kept telling myself over and over, "You don't actually like singing." I know that's not the truth, but that made it easier for me to imagine myself somewhere else completely. Now that I think about it, I bet Sofie was doing the same thing when her eyes were closed.

Gina, of course, was so loud and had the spot right in front of me for the concert. She sings super-duper good. One time at Girl Scouts camp, everybody even lined up by the bathroom door just to hear her shower voice. I wonder what it's like to have people want to listen to you all the time. Today I noticed that she still wears the friendship charm bracelet I used to be a part of. I don't even know what happened to my half, but I hated that I had to listen hers jingle all afternoon long.

I just wish that she would say "I'm sorry." I don't think that she ever will, though. Gina's house has a sauna in the backyard, but for sure not a trampoline. All I'm saying is that she probably doesn't want to be kicked out of the Trampoline Club either. Either way, pretending to do the Jingle Bells' "fa la la la's" backup for her made me swallow and swallow like a fish out of water. I almost forgot that I was surrounded by people.

Sorry to say, but I think Mr. B noticed me and Sofie not participating like we should. He scratched his beard all of a sudden and said, "Ellie, Sofie, I want to hear your voices."

My old friends giggled at hearing our names next to each other like that. I wish Mr. B had given them the stink eye, but instead he and the music teacher gave us both solos in the next song. Sofie is a great singer, but I can't believe the teachers thought that I could be big in that way. Don't they know that the gym has echoes in it, and that makes everything extra, extra loud? Singing about the "fourth day of Christmas" was not the miracle I had in mind. I tried to peek at Sofie again to see if she was okay with our new assignment. Again, I could see nothing but the side of Dylan's head.

The song came on next from the little boom box, and my turn to sing came too quickly. I opened my mouth and looked around the room. I wanted there to be at least one person looking at me with nice eyes, but the audience was empty and all I could feel was Dylan rolling his eyes at me. I swear it was a nightmare. I had to sing "On the fourth day of Christmas my true love gave to me four calling birds" loud enough for everybody to hear. I don't even want to think about the "true love" who gets all of these presents. I can't believe I have to do it all again tomorrow for even more people to roll their eyes at me.

At the end of rehearsal, I looked for Sofie in the crowds of chatty friends, but she was already gone and probably started walking home without me. If she hadn't been singing "seven swans a-swimming" over and over again, I wouldn't have believed she was there at all. I hope she sleeps okay. I got her a really nice rock for her porch today, even though I know it's probably not enough.

Sorry, thanks for listening,
Ellie

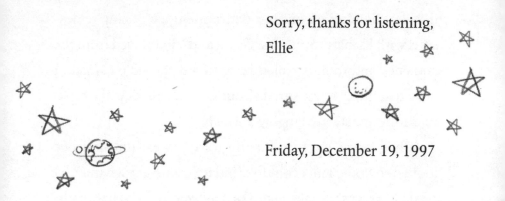

Friday, December 19, 1997

Hello,

I hope you like this special gold balloon. Finding it at the reception table was one of the only things I actually liked about the winter concert tonight.

Before the show even started, a bunch of kids were peeking between the heavy cafeteria doors to see whose parents came. I looked at the growing crowd for just half a second, but I couldn't care less about my dad not being there. He was busy hunting elk in his orange hat instead, plus he only cares about me when it's super late at night. Sofie, on the other hand, didn't even try to see all the families showing up in the cafeteria. She leaned against the brick wall and said, "Who gets in such big trouble for having covered lights anyways?" She has a really good point there. What made me really sad though was when she said, "I don't care about the carriage car anymore."

That night she sang the quietest I've ever heard her sing. It's like she blocked out her entire memory of singing lessons with Richard. Still, Mrs. Gavia and Viivi waved from the audience and took her picture with a disposable camera. I have to admit, I never cared about the seventh day of Christmas until she started singing about it.

When it was my turn for the solo, I swear the audience looked so bored and I couldn't find my mom anywhere. All I could hear was the fake piano on the tape and Dylan breathing, he might have even said the bad words *shut up* to me. I wonder if that counts as him talking to me and breaking the Trampoline Club rules. I can't even remember if anybody clapped for me. I kind of blacked that out too. I just know that Nathan Lucas got a bigger applause, and he lives all the way in Calumet.

Just between us, I ran to my special bathroom stall to cry as soon as the song was over. I locked the door behind me tight, and took off my headband. I hope I didn't disappoint Mr. B for skipping the "Silent Night" finale. I just don't know what sound came out of me. I don't know if my voice was any good. I remember Sofie told me once when we were practicing our confident walks, "You can be yourself around me." Sometimes I don't know what it means to be myself anymore, but she made a flower bouquet out of bunched-up toilet paper with a twist at the end. It was the most beautiful thing I have ever seen.

Tonight I made my own toilet paper bouquet. I held it on my lap while my nose dripped onto my fancy black pants. Sofie is the only person who really hears me speak anymore. I'm not sure if that makes her lucky or not. What do you do when your nose won't stop dripping and you know that people are waiting for you? Even Sofie's baby sister made it through the concert without crying.

When I heard some noise coming from the hallway, I forced myself to unlock the stall door. I crumpled up my bouquet and looked into the mirror. My eyes were all green and red, just in time for Christmas. It was like I wasn't even looking at myself. My thoughts just kept getting louder. I had to put my hands under that noisy dryer to make them go all quiet. I stayed standing under the heat until my palms started to sweat and change colors. Maybe there was at least one person who thought my solo was beautiful enough. I mostly hope that people will just forget about it by the time winter break ends. Sometimes I'm just scared of breaking every rule and every promise.

As soon as I got back to the gym, Mom found me right away and took way too many pictures. My eyes were still all red, but she made me say "cheese" and "girl power" in a group photo with the Trampoline Club. Courtney made a peace sign, but I'm sure she didn't mean it. I was wearing my old headband and everything, but does Mom really think that nothing has changed? I smiled through it anyways.

What bothered me even more was that Dylan probably didn't even care about the fact I left the concert early. He and his friends were too busy with their hacky sacks and Hawaiian fruit punch. I only got close enough to hear them say "waazzzup?" over and over again, even though none of them would ever actually answer the question. What's even worse than that, I didn't see Sofie anywhere in the crowd. She wasn't near the table of ranch dressing and oatmeal cookies either. The gym was full, but it sure felt empty to me.

Some Girl Scout's mom then got on the loudspeaker and told everyone to stand in a circle and hold hands. That didn't help anything. Now I remember why I quit Girl Scouts. We had to sing, "Make new friends, but keep the old, one is silver and the other's gold. A circle's round, it has no end, that's how long I want to be your friend." I don't actually know what that song is called, but everybody knows it. It's not supposed to be a sad song, but I looked around the circle and my only friend wasn't there.

I hope somebody nice finds this balloon mail because I have a big favor to ask you. There are only a few days left, but could you try sending something to Richard in time for Christmas? He taught Sofie how to use her whole voice, and I love her voice even when she sings at her quietest. Baby Viivi doesn't even really have a voice yet, but I bet hers will be great too.

Sofie told me he's at the county jail. It would be great if you could mail him a snow globe or a jar of honey, or get him a new light since that's kind of why he's in there to begin with. You can also just make a card with a nice note, like I did the other day. His name is Richard Gavia, but some people call him Rich. I just wrote in his letter, "Sofie loves you, and hasn't forgotten about you." You can write the same thing in your letter if you're feeling stuck. I just can't believe I didn't share that Kit Kat bar with him when I had the chance.

I think I'm going to light a candle for him at church if my mom lets me. Do you go to church? Mine is kind of funny, but maybe it's normal. It's skinny with white siding, like a bigger version of our house, and it's just a little bit outside of Houghton. I will probably have to be there a lot over the next few days for Christmas stuff, which means I will light a lot of candles.

If you do decide to try to light your own candle, you should know that there are a few Catholic rules. First, make sure you wear a dress if people think you're a girl, and nice pants are for boys. Then make sure you put the oil water on your forehead when you come in, and kneel and think about life and all your problems when they tell you to. You'll probably hear some old stories with no endings from the priest, and then you say the words *and also with you* at the same time as everyone else. Also, eat bread, even when it's not real bread, and put a few dollars in the basket even if you don't have enough for yourself. Some of the music is pretty good, though I usually just move my lips. For some reason nobody ever claps for the band at the end.

If other families smile at you and want to shake your hand with "Peace be with you," then you know you're doing a good job. I have to admit, it would be really nice to have a reminder that I'm good while I'm there.

I hope you have a good night, a better one than this.

Sincerely,
Rowan

Tuesday, December 23, 1997

Hi.

I'm feeling good about winter break so far. I have had more time to ice-skate and work on my refrigerator box art. Dad doesn't get back from his second round of elk hunting until tomorrow, so my mom and I have been watching movies he doesn't like. I especially like watching *Baby, Take a Bow* and the other Shirley Temple ones with her. They make her laugh, and she always hums along to that "Animal Crackers" song in *Curly Top*. I don't see her like that very much, so it's nice.

When Mom went out to shovel snow, I watched the last episode of *Boy Meets World*. Cory and Topanga decided their differences made them stronger. He then sang her a Christmas carol, even when he doesn't like singing. I don't know, it gave me hope. Maybe Dylan will learn to appreciate our differences too.

Also, you know what else? During a commercial break, I snooped under the Christmas tree and noticed there are way more boxes for me than I expected. I know what I really want won't fit into a box, but fingers-crossed a haircut works out anyways.

Thanks,
Rowan

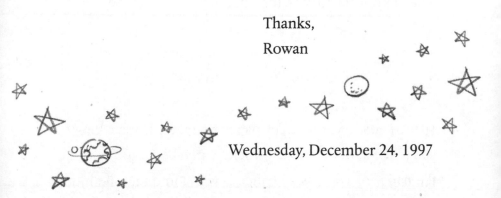

Wednesday, December 24, 1997

Hi.

I know it's almost Christmas and things are supposed to be perfect and all, but I can't sleep. I usually can help myself fall asleep by reaching under my quilt, under my nightshirt, and feel for my ribs in the dark. The bones on my sides remind me that I have a body and that something is holding me up. Sometimes when I can't find my ribs, I get scared that my body is gone somehow and I will just disappear. Do you know what I mean? I don't know, sorry.

What I'm trying to say is that I really need to know somebody is actually reading my balloon letters. I don't know what would make me special enough to have a guardian angel, but if I do please give me a sign. Some people around here actually like to say "Even my guardian angel drinks." If that's what you're too busy doing like my dad, then please stop. Maybe write me a letter instead? Sorry, I don't know what it's normal to wish for anymore.

Sincerely,
Rowan

PS, I made you a toilet paper bouquet. I don't know if you'll like it, but it's your present. I attached it to the end of the balloon. There is a chance it will come undone by the time it gets to you, but now you know what it is in case anybody asks. Just make sure you don't water it like a normal flower. I watered a little bit of it by accident, but you should know that it will only stay alive if you keep it dry. I hope you have a very Merry Christmas. Bye.

Hi,

For Christmas, I got the game Trouble, a pillow with Casper the Friendly Ghost's face on it, and some other things I can't remember right now. To be honest with you, I miss school. I miss the water fountains, the hallways with inspirational sayings everywhere. I wouldn't even mind seeing the back of Courtney's head right now. Church is long and winter is long. Nights are long, and there are only so many balloons I can buy. I hope your winter break is going well if you have one. I'm just not feeling so sure about mine anymore.

Dad slept in my room again. He said yard work is hurting his back, but really he's just much older than most dads. His forehead has a lot of lines on it and his body left a shadow shaped like a turtle on my wall when I was half-asleep. There's something about my bright pink walls that seem to glow in the dark. I wonder if my dad thinks I glow in the dark too, because he always seems to find me no matter what. Patti, Pouch, Pinchers, Legs, and all of my other stuffed animals were smart and ran to the floor.

I still think of myself as a boy, but I really hope I don't grow up to be my dad. I hope there are more choices. It was really hard to fall back asleep thinking about it. Making my own shadow puppet of a dog and a rabbit with my hands didn't help, neither did feeling for my ribs again, so I tiptoed my way out. I stepped over all four Beanie Babies, my new Casper the Friendly Ghost pillow, two pairs of pants. I got to the hallway and went down the stairs, passed my mom quietly smoking a cigarette in the kitchen, and finally made it here. Here's a map.

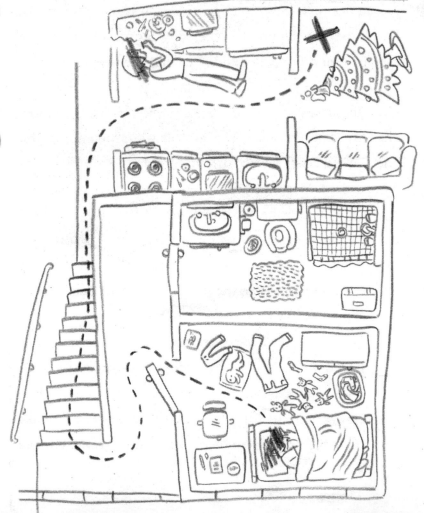

I should just be grateful for having my dad at all. I should feel lucky that he's not in jail or anything like that, but I don't know. I hope it's okay that I'm telling you this.

Right now I am sitting in a nice space between our Christmas tree and the wall, just like Sofie has at her house. You should try it where you live too. It feels safe behind the tree because I know it will always glow in the dark brighter than me. It actually stands almost the exact same height as my dad. He's just tall enough to make eye contact with the gold angel that lives on top. I bet the angel would have a thing or two to say to him. One day, I'll be tall enough for the angel to see me better.

I've never actually written a letter from back here before, but I just discovered that there's actually enough space for me to stretch out my legs. The glass ornaments ding whenever my Scooby pajama pants brush by them and I can see my face in their round reflections. The only downside is that my hair keeps getting caught in the plastic tree branches.

I didn't get a haircut for Christmas, but I am thinking about just cutting it all by myself. Have you ever gotten yourself a gift? Dad for sure got himself that orange drill and Johnny Cash wall calendar, and the year before this one too. To be honest, I just wanted a different world for Christmas. Sofie and I tried to give each other something as close to that as we could. I came up with the idea for us to make each other paper airplanes that carry maps to our favorite places. She put all of hers into a green shoebox. Inside were directions to the summer carnival Ferris wheel, the Copper Country Mall arcade, her mom's whitefish soup recipe, and some other places too. My most favorite one of all shows how to get to our giant recess rock. She talked about it like it was as special as the moon.

I wrapped her gift with real maps from New York City that I found in my mom's car. I've never actually been there before, but it sure sounds nice in every movie I've seen. Have you ever been there? I heard that there is a Ferris wheel and a beach, and even a Rainforest Cafe too. Maybe one day when I'm old enough, I'll drive to New York in an RV and live there. I don't know. I want to live somewhere that feels not so heavy. I would live there with Sofie, and it wouldn't have to be a secret. Do you ever think about running away too? Even if it's to a place that maybe doesn't exist? Like an imaginary world on a snowflake, or a big silver-and-white ballroom where you could swing from chandeliers and a wear tinfoil hat? Even New York feels like a little imaginary dream or something.

It might sound silly, but Sofie was in the dream I had last week. We laid in two separate beds on an iced-over lake just strong enough to hold us both. We pulled the blankets off, looked inside our belly buttons and pretended they were wishing wells. She asked right away, "What did you wish for?" She actually asked two times in a row and I had to tell her "That's bad luck" because it is.

I can't really remember what I wished for in my dream. Sometimes I'm not even so sure what I'm allowed to wish for. I've mostly written about wishes about Dylan, but I don't know. It's not like he wants me around. I really wish I didn't still have a crush on him, but I do. He makes me feel at home in a weird way, but the weirder thing is that I don't even like my house that much.

This is kind of embarrassing to ask, but can a crush make me feel big? Like, have you ever had a friend you didn't really have the right word for? Someone who makes you feel strong and warm, like a close-feeling feeling-close to a girl that's your friend? I don't know. I have big feelings with Sofie. Whenever she is here, the ship we built out of the refrigerator box feels as quiet as the falling snow. It's dear, like a dear, dear home that we built all by ourselves.

I just hope Sofie never reads this. I hope that none of my old friends read this either. I wouldn't be allowed to go under a trampoline for the rest of my life. So, whoever you are, please promise that you will burn this letter when you're done reading it. Either way, writing this has made me feel a million times better. I was really starting to feel bad for myself for not knowing more shadow puppets.

I'm going to go back to sleep now.

Thanks,
Rowan Beck

Monday, December 29, 1997

Hi.

On the way home from ice-skating with my parents today, I saw the black cloud of smoke toward Dollar Bay and I imagined that someone actually burned my last letter after all. For that minute, it made me feel less alone.

I saw the smoke at the perfect time actually because skating today was a little weird. I saw Mary, Gina, and Courtney with some other girls from class. Maybe they are all new to the Trampoline Club too. They were mostly busy showing off the fact that they have enough friends to spell out all of "YMCA" with their arms. I did like going backward and doing a few twirls on the ice when nobody was looking. I practiced a few hockey moves too, but I don't know. There must be more to life.

Not to complain, but this week off school is already feeling like forever and a half. I hope Sofie is okay too. Some things have been happening with her, and I'm not sure how to talk about it yet. In the meantime, I hope you also find a nice window to look out of.

Sincerely,
Rowan Beck

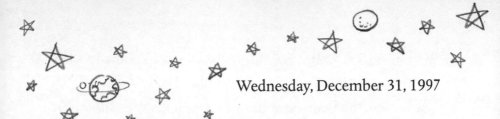

Hello Friend,

This balloon is from the cashier at Freedom Valu's. He gave
it to me for free with a smile even bigger than his mustache. I
went there with my mom earlier today so she could get cham-
pagne "just in case we have company over," which everybody
knows wasn't going to happen. She also got her radio bingo
cards and even a few Club Reno lottery tickets too. There was
the longest line ever, I guess everybody was getting things to
celebrate with and take chances on. It's about eleven o'clock
right now, and I bet all of those people are now sitting around
clocks waiting for 1998 to start. I bet most of them want to
have do-overs, kiss someone on the lips, or tell a secret. I'm
not sure if I want to do any of those things, though. Do you?

I'm just trying my best to feel good about this next year
because last New Year's Eve I got to do the countdown with
my old BFFs at Courtney's house. We filmed ourselves drinking sparkling apple juice and throwing confetti in the air, and
then we all slept side by side. I don't know, do you think it's
possible to not think about what other people are doing?
This year I want to scream in a different way. I sat on top of
the stairs and listened to Dad give his usual "I'm doing my

139

best" speech over the ball drop special on TV. I made a big decision right then.

I locked the bathroom door and practiced smiling into the medicine cabinet mirror. It wasn't working so well, so I decided that it was time to give myself the gift that I have been wanting for so many Christmases in a row. I cut my own hair. It was like a movie watching the strands fall in slow motion onto the tile. I liked how it felt, so I kept going and going with my yellow craft scissors. I cut it all the way to my shoulders, just long enough to make the tiniest ponytail, the size of a paintbrush.

I was already feeling a little bit lighter, but I had to stop before I could give myself bangs. My mom started knocking real loud on the door. It was like thunder. Her voice filled the whole room and she wasn't even inside of it. I just don't see why she got so mad at me for cutting my hair when she always makes the New Year about losing weight. As soon as I stepped out of the bathroom, Mom said, "Go to your room. You're grounded." I still don't think I actually did anything wrong. Has that happened to you before?

I thought about keeping my head under the quilt until it's the new millennium or something. That way, I could just enjoy my new haircut without having to worry about anyone watching. The heat of my own breath made me feel trapped, though, and it was dark under the blanket with no stars at all. It didn't take long for me to totally give up on hiding. I let in some light and fresh air, and you know what? I haven't stopped brushing my fingers through my hair since. I actually think I want to make it shorter, even though Shirley Temple is the only girl I know with hair like that.

I'm trying my best to not let anything take my smile away since it's supposed to be a day to celebrate beginnings and watch Dick Clark on TV. I actually cut all of the knots away too. It's so nice to have them gone, even if it means that I'm grounded for it. I do wish that I could show my haircut right now to someone who cares, though. Mr. B once told the class: "If you ever feel alone, you should call someone." It's funny Mr. B said that while handing out our emergency contact forms. I've never written down an emergency contact who could help me when I'm feeling lonely. I just put some adult's name.

When I feel alone, I never tell another person. Instead, I usually hum to myself or I look for leftover pizza in the refrigerator. Other times, I sit with the skates and shoes inside my closet because sometimes it's nice to feel small surrounded by small things.

To be honest, I wouldn't even know what to say to an emergency contact if I called them, especially when it's so close to the most special midnight of the year. I'd want to say something simple like "I feel alone," but that's probably not an emergency at all. Maybe that person would laugh at me for trying, and say I'm a big waste of time. Maybe they will say that I should have tried harder in 1997.

In the meantime, I'm realizing that sometimes just sitting together is enough. Sofie and I tried to sit and breathe together on her big orange couch at the beginning of break. I told Sofie about how I got caught trying to pee standing up at my house. Mom knocked loud and said it's time that I do something right for a change. She was so happy watching Shirley Temple movies before Dad came home. When I told Sofie all that, she let out a breath so big that I could feel it traveling all the way from her belly.

Then it was Sofie's turn to cry. She told me that her dad got into another fight with someone in charge and is going to be sent to Marquette Hickory Prison. I don't really understand the whole thing, but I do know that he is farther away from Sofie than ever before. I also know that he is in bigger trouble than ever too. Like I said, I don't really know how to talk about these things. It's bad to say "no" to the wrong people. Sorry. It's just that holidays are supposed to be a happy time, but I'm not so sure about that anymore.

Sofie and I had made a special card for her dad a few weeks ago. I hope it got to him before he was moved to this new place. It had a drawing of two bears sharing a jar of honey, which I hear is good for your voice. I hope that one day he gets to make something out of the wood he used to chop down. I hope he knows that we forgive him for whatever happened. I hope for so many things.

Sofie forgot to breathe for a few seconds when she talked

about it. She said, "Maybe I should go away too." I hugged her tight right then and there. I started to sing her my own version of "You Are My Sunshine." It was louder and truer than anything that came out of me at the winter concert. I guess somehow everything feels a little safer in basements. I stayed in the hug long enough for her to drift asleep. I put my ear on her back. It was like listening to Lake Superior with each breath coming in like a bigger wave. I let my head rise and fall with her.

I actually thought about calling Sofie on the phone tonight for New Year's, but she wouldn't even be able to see my haircut. She's probably busy anyway, sitting with her mom next to the clock, counting down for something good to happen.

By the way, I just looked out my bedroom window because I heard Jax barking. It's now midnight. The sky is full of red and silver fireworks, changing into blue and some other colors too. Their bursts look like the kind of dandelions you can wish on. Maybe that means something good is going to happen after all. I'll try to make a wish, and you can too.

Happy New Year to you, friend.

Sincerely,
Rowan

Hi.

All week long, I've been waking up at four in the morning. There is for sure nobody I can call that late at night to talk about feeling alone and weird. Sometimes I just try to pass the time in my refrigerator box.

Luckily, this morning I let myself stay in bed and fall back into a dream for a little bit. I lived in the sky with the fireworks, but I was watching my body sleep in Portage Lake. My head was just above the water. A blue boat full of bearded men in yellow hats fished nearby, and they let me stay exactly how I was. We all just did our own thing as the flashing fireworks kept changing the colors of everything. It was nice.

Anyways, I have to go do more chores now. Mom and Dad are nervous that our pipes are going to break because it has been so cold, but I don't know. I think it will be all okay.

Sincerely,
Rowan

Hi.

I have to tell somebody this. My parents tried to take my refrigerator box away. They took it to the street folded in half. They said, "It's in the way." Mom has a New Year's resolution to get rid of "what we don't need." If that's true, why are they keeping my first-grade finger-paints or piles of green, coppery rocks from White Pine? Geez Louise, all of those just sit in their own dusty boxes.

I can't tell my parents what the box means to me, so instead I just did what they said, and finished my "you're grounded for cutting your own hair" chores. They just don't get it.

You have to swear on your life to keep quiet about this. While shoveling the driveway this afternoon, I came up with an idea for a secret mission to take my box back. I kept my face buried in my SpaghettiOs dinner, then watched out my bedroom window until I heard the TV turn off. I tucked the little amount of hair I have left into my hat, and snuck out the front door as quiet as I could. I brushed off the new snow, and was so strong that I lifted the cardboard over my head. I promise you, my refrigerator box is not in the way. It's my way out. It's my ship.

The box is now folded, safe in the way deep back of my closet. It won't be staying there forever.

Rowan

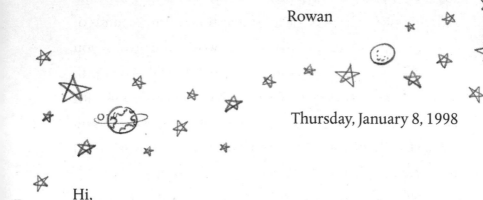

Thursday, January 8, 1998

Hi,

Winter break is over and I'm officially not grounded anymore. It's because I took down the Christmas tree and put the ornaments and angel into a box without anybody asking me to. My parents told me I did a good job doing extra chores. I left it at that and kept my mouth shut for the rest of our hot dog and orange pop dinner. I usually have a lot of secrets at the dinner table, but lately I have a few more.

On Monday after school, I brought my refrigerator box to Sofie's house so she could keep it safe. I guess it's good Sofie gets another favorite place, but she never asked why I gave it to her. We unfolded the cardboard together and spent a whole entire day inside our ship drawing, eating sourdough sandwiches, and playing checkers without talking about it at all. Sofie has a superpower where she only asks questions when she really means them. I think that's better than having the powers that most people want, like turning invisible or flying away. She asks the most questions during rounds of truth or truth. Questions like, "What would you grow if you had seeds for anything in the world?" or "What do you think about the neighbor's new fence?" She once asked me with really wide eyes, "If you could fill your body with anything other than blood, what would it be?" That was a hard one. I think I would like to be filled with maple syrup or snow.

She never once asked me why I called myself a boy yesterday.

We were sitting outside of the box to watch *James and the Giant Peach* and play Jenga. The narrator said that James used to be the loneliest boy there was, and now has a loving new family and all the friends in the world. I put another wood block on top of our block-stacking game, and told Sofie, "I'm a boy. I know it." It was my first time saying those words out loud in a strong way, in a way I never told the Trampoline Club.

You don't hate me, right? I really did mean what I said to Sofie, but I got scared for a minute. I put another block on top of our tower, and could hardly trust that either. It was almost forty stories high, and having only two blocks on the very bottom wasn't very much support at all. The tower wiggled and waved. My shoulders crept up expecting that it would fall any second. Even worse than losing the game would have been Sofie telling me to leave because I said the wrong thing. I couldn't help but think about us breaking up, and Mrs. Gavia taking my box back out to the street.

Before anything bad happened, Sofie took the movie out of the VCR and flopped onto the orange couch. The cushions looked soft enough to disappear into. I slowly joined her on the one farthest from her. I kept my arms folded and my feet buried. I was afraid of her questions, that I'd get too scared to repeat myself. I'm not even totally sure what it means to be a boy, so don't ask me. But haven't you ever said something about yourself and it's like you can feel your heart beating for the first time in your life? It's like that.

Lucky for me, Sofie didn't do that. She also didn't give a big speech saying "I don't care" or "It doesn't change anything about us." That's good because I want her to care about the ways I sometimes hurt and change. Instead, she just said, "You are a boy, and I'm glad you met yourself."

Then she said, "You can stay here too, whenever you want to." Listening to her words made my shoulders creep down. I felt okay enough to stretch out my legs again. Our toes touched from opposite ends of the couch and we shared small smiles. She's right, I did meet myself.

You still like me, right? I hope so, because I like me right now too. Just like James in the movie, I'm not meant to be miserable either.

Hope you're also having a good day today.

Sincerely,
Me

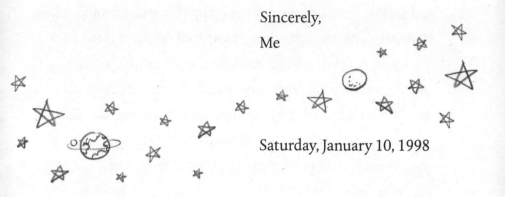

Saturday, January 10, 1998

Dear Whoever You Are,

I finally went to a slumber party, but I wasn't exactly invited to it. It's hard to explain. I'm actually at it right now.

You should know that this might be my last letter. Things are changing fast, and honestly I didn't know how hard finding a good home was going to be. In *James and the Giant Peach*, it took James running away and turning into a cartoon to do that. I promise you that I didn't really want to run away. It's just that my house door is locked right now. I'm just glad I saved my refrigerator box when I did.

I tried to say "I'm a boy" in a not so strong way at my house this morning. I was just trying to cut my hair again. I was tired of it covering my ears, but, even in the movie, James's aunts said that dreaming could get him killed. It's all my fault, isn't it? I feel so stupid. I just really hope nobody catches me crying like this and tells me I'm not a real boy.

I should have hid everything I cut off better. I should not have left all the strands I threw away looking like a bird's nest sitting on top of the wastebasket. I should not have skipped making my bed this morning. I also should not have accidentally knocked over my orange juice at our special Pillsbury cinnamon roll breakfast. Most of all, I should not have gone outside to check for the mail when Mom went out for her errands.

I walked away from the mailbox with empty hands. This time, I admit that it would have been really nice to have an early valentine or balloons or a warm scarf to hold at that very moment. The front door wouldn't open. I knocked on it for forever. I know it's not allowed, but I even kicked the door trying to get it to open for me. Dad was for sure inside because I could hear Mr. Karl Bohnak talk about the cold front on TV, and I even heard the microwave heating something up when I first came down the stairs. This one time Dad threw all my shoes into the snow because I put them in the wrong spot by the door, but I never thought it would be me getting left out in the snow.

I don't understand. He was trying to be so nice to me last night, but it was so chilly out there on the porch that it hurt. I didn't care anymore about looking at my breath, and instead thought about my hands freezing off completely. My ears actually felt the cold more than ever because I had no hair to keep them warm. I really had no choice but to walk to Sofie's house. I probably stomped on top of so many snowflakes on my way there. Imagine how many worlds got totally crushed on that walk alone.

I'm probably asking you too much, but do you think anything will go back to how it was before? I want it to, but I also don't want it to. I hope I don't have to stop being Rowan from now on. Do I have to be Ellie to be good? I don't know anything anymore.

When I got to Sofie's creaky red door, her mom's eyes looked like glass. She let me inside, and said, "Oh, Ellie. I'm surprised to see you here. Sofie was just thinking about calling you." I closed the door behind me softly to keep more snow from avalanching off the roof. I took off my icy tennis shoes first thing. They flopped to the ground, ready to melt. Sofie hopped off of the tall kitchen chair, and said, "Hi, Rowan." She didn't bother to finish reading her Garfield comics.

Dusty the cat followed us into the basement, and I made myself into a mountain with a dozen quilts on top. The couch sank in like it remembered me. It felt good to be remembered by something so soft, to feel my toes again.

Sofie was really excited to have company, I think. As soon as I got warm and settled, Sofie asked me a million things, like "Do you want to play Jenga again?" "Do you want to play cribbage?" "Do you want to play house?" I know that she meant every question, but I said no to it all. I felt bad and I felt nothing at the same time. She then asked if I wanted to do something extra-extra fun, like sledding in Swedetown or renting free kids movies from Family Video's. I said no again and again. I had trouble saying yes to anything that whole afternoon, even to playing with the box that I tried so hard to save.

I still feel so bad about it because I know Sofie feels alone in the world too, especially now. I hope she's not mad at me. It's just that sometimes when I get really sad, I can only think about whales and imaginary places that are so far away. I got totally lost just staring at the wall until Sofie moved a few inches closer to me. I liked the feeling of her being closer, but it made me even more nervous. I didn't want to get in trouble for something all over again. I can't deal with any more trouble. She put her head on my shoulder, but I didn't feel it at all. I might as well have been somewhere else. I might as well have been gone. Do you think I'm a bad friend?

I guess I'm just bad at slumber parties. Especially now I heard that the Trampoline Club is also going by the name Lambda Kappa Kappa, or something like that, because one day they want to live in that pink Greek house with white pillars next to the big river. I like that house too. I have driven past it a million times and it's giant. I bet I could have my own room inside of it, but I don't know. Maybe I will have to be called Ellie to stay anywhere at all.

I like Sofie's house and everything, but now I just want to

go home. I should probably go look for her. Viivi started crying more than an hour ago, and I haven't seen either of them since.

I don't want to be a boy anymore. I wish I knew how to make it stop. I wish I was easier to take care of.

Sorry,
Ellie

Sunday, January 11, 1998

Hi.

I'm back in my bed in the pink room in the white house with the frozen lawn. Everything is where I left it, but it somehow doesn't feel right. Maybe I should just be grateful, but I don't know. My parents are talking downstairs. They keep using the word "problem," and for once they aren't talking about each other. They are talking about me. I wish I could tell them that they are wrong.

I don't even know how they figured out I was at Sofie's. Either way, it was really nice of Mrs. Gavia to let me stay over last night. I'm glad to know that I'm not banned from

153

sleepovers for forever, but I do wish it had been on purpose enough to get a party invitation in the mail. Truth is, I didn't sleep so well on Sofie's basement floor. I stayed up super late thinking about that locked front door, but I was also thinking about how nice the pillowcase felt on my neck. It was cold, but in a good way. My shorter-than-ever hair lets me feel things I have never felt before. You know what I mean? I actually really like it. I'll try to explain it better once I have it all figured out more.

Sofie and I then spent all morning doing stuff for school. Don't judge me, but I didn't have my backpack with me before I got locked out. I had to look at Sofie's worksheets and books to fill out my own answers onto a loose-leaf piece of paper. I skipped filling out my name. I chewed on my pencil and crossed out most of the answers I tried to write down. The multiple choice questions were the hardest of all, and by the time I opened Sofie's science workbook, I just stared at it. We just started learning about the human body. It's complicated and there are a lot of parts to learn. I still can't even think about that right now. I've been getting tired of answering other people's questions lately. Mr. B might be disappointed, but I decided to skip science homework altogether. I put the workbook back inside of Sofie's backpack. For the first time in my life, I didn't care about getting an incomplete.

Sofie was still working at that point, so I tried turning

my brain off for once and used Sofie's backpack as a pillow. The cushion was kind of stiff and the zipper's jingling made it impossible to nap, but I did have a nice view of the space underneath Sofie's couch. I could see two blocks, three quarters, enough to buy a carton of chocolate milk, and lots of dust bunnies.

I'm not a bad student, I swear. I was just tired, and didn't want to do this science stuff on my own and I don't really want the reward of being a hall cop or hall monitor or whatever anyways. I used to be so good, and sometimes I'm not so sure if I ever will be again.

All of a sudden, Sofie rolled a permanent marker toward me and said, "Do you want to play a game?" I said, "As long as it's a game that we could both win." She nodded, and I scooped up the marker she gave me. The two of us came up with an idea to write our initials onto one of the wooden legs of the couch. Do you know that game? It's okay if you don't because I think we just made it up out of nowhere today. It's called tree trunk.

We knelt down to the carpet like we were about to pray. Even though I helped make up the game, I had no idea what I was doing. I have never written something permanent in a permanent place before. I just sat there with the marker for who knows how long. I wonder if it is that hard for the people who write in the bathroom stalls at school. Sofie then reminded me, "You can use the name Rowan if you want to."

It was the first time I smiled with teeth showing all weekend long. I even challenged myself to write in cursive R.B. for Rowan Beck.

The blue marker moved smoothly and I made loops in each letter like I really meant it. Sofie wrote her initials, S.G., right next to mine, and put a plus sign in between them. "R.B. + S.G." was like a cool math problem where we add to each other. We both stared at it for a long time, but not in a way where we were trying to solve it.

Sofie sat up and she said, "It's like a valentine." It was so quiet and loud at the same time when she told me that. What do you think she meant by it? Maybe I should try to get her something. Everyone in class has to give everyone a valentine, so it's not that weird, right? I don't know. I guess I have about a month to figure it all out.

It was hard to say goodbye to Sofie and that basement couch after that. Apparently my mom had called Sofie's mom, and they decided I had to come home after the slumber party. Mom drove over to pick me up like she was doing me some big favor. I had hardly any time to get ready. I didn't have a coat to put on, so I just I crinkled up my last few homework papers and stuffed them into my pocket.

On the ride back to the house, Mom kept on talking in a weird, squeaky voice. She even wore her BE HAPPY shirt with sequins sewn on front. She said, "I've been making some calls, and we're going to do something fun together next Sunday." She looked at me through the rear-view mirror, and was not smiling when she said "It's going to be really good." I wonder what it's going to be. Do you think she wants to do something fun with Ellie or Rowan? Maybe she found out that Dad is going out of town for hunting, so then we can watch old movies again? I'm just confused about the whole thing because normally we all go to church Sundays and I have never been allowed to do something else instead.

Of course, we didn't talk about what really happened this weekend. When we got back home, Mom, Dad, and I shoveled the roof, snow-scooped the driveway, and then we all three watched TV together for once. It was a new episode of *America's Funniest Home Videos*, but I feel like I had seen it before. Someone fell off of a trampoline, and someone else got bit by a dog. Mom laughed as her BE HAPPY sequins bounced light around the room. Maybe she doesn't know what really happened yesterday either. I mean, she was doing errands after all. Dad had a small smile and drank something that was see-through even though the bottle said it was fruit flavored. I guess they're both happy now, but I would have liked it better if my dad had said that he was sorry for locking the door on me.

I spent a lot of the TV show imagining myself building a snowman outside of the window instead. Of course, I couldn't tell my parents I would rather build a snowman by myself instead of sitting there with them. We haven't made one together in such a long time, not since we lived in White Pine and had a dog of our own.

Maybe my dad really didn't mean to lock me out. Maybe he will come to my room and say that he still likes me. I wouldn't mind that if it meant that things were going to be okay from now on. I did notice that the wastebasket I put all my hairs into was sitting next to the TV instead of its usual spot in the bathroom, so I don't know.

I guess, for now, it is kind of nice being back in my own room with its own door and its own window. The first thing I did was make my bed. After that, I pulled out my art supplies to draw two big pictures of Sofie's couch. One of the drawings is actually for you.

SoFie's couch

I want you to have it because I think you could fall in love with that couch too. Who knows? Maybe I'll open a museum of drawings one day. In the meantime, I taped the other couch drawing next to my bed. That way, I won't have to travel so far to feel safe and soft.

Sincerely,
Me

Monday, January 19, 1998

Hello Out There,

Nobody complimented my haircut at school and my confident walk was really pathetic, even when Sofie called me a "he." Usually hearing her say that makes me feel good, but I don't know.

I have to tell you that Sunday with Mom and Dad wasn't fun at all. I sat in the backseat with the dirty swamper boots, and ice that somehow grew inside the car windows. We pulled out of the driveway through a white-out of falling snow. We passed right by the full parking lot at church, and I was so surprised. I started hoping right away that we were going to ski jump on Porcupine Mountains or find an ice fishing tournament. Instead, we kept on driving, past the old Quincey Mine, through the town that everyone says has thirteen bars and two churches. We went so far that there were no more car dealerships, drive-throughs, motels, or anything I am used to.

On the way there, Mom said, "I'm so proud of you," and she never says that. Dad only said his usual rant about the government sending the wrong people to fix our problems, and that he thinks maybe the Michigan Militia will help us get rid of those people.

I just hope I can be good, and no one has to send the Michigan Militia on me. I hope the door will stay open for me. I don't know. I have to do this new thing every Sunday now. I have to sit in a room with someone who pretends to listen. I don't really get it, but I think you should know that maybe it's best you call me Ellie from now on.

Sincerely,

Me, I guess

Hello,

Sorry I didn't write a letter last week. Instead of buying my usual chocolate milk and balloon, I got a deep-fried Oreo at the winter carnival. I ate the whole thing in just two bites while watching broom ball matches between friends that aren't mine. They were laughing a lot, probably college students. I didn't stay to see who won the game. I walked around Mont Ripley and saw a bunch of people I knew, and a bunch of people I didn't know. I saw all kinds of fireworks and bonfires too, but none of them made me feel closer to anyone.

Is it possible to miss yourself? It's weird to say this, but I kind of miss myself. It's kind of like working hard to shovel the sidewalk, and then a big noisy plow comes by and fills everything back in. Do you know what I mean? Dad says I'm supposed to grow out my hair. He's extra mean to me now that it's short, but he still visits me in my room just as much as before. Sometimes I don't know if he loves me or if he hates me. Anyways, I wanted to send you a drawing of what my hair looks like right now, just how I like it, before it goes on changing again.

You should know that I haven't really been talking to Sofie ever since our surprise slumber party. Both my parents think that Sofie is actually making me worse and Mom thinks she's the reason I ran away. Mom says, "You are too easily influenced by your friends." Mom says, "I don't want you to regret anything" like she does. It really can't be true, can it? I didn't run away. The door was locked with Dad inside. I don't know.

I have been holding my pee all day long so I don't see Sofie in the bathroom for our confident walk meetings. I'm not happy about it, but maybe the other kids at school will notice and want to be the kind of friends I'm supposed to have. I would even go along with talking about the Green Bay Packers at the Super Bowl if that's what everybody else wants to talk about. I don't know, I just feel so bad about everything at school, at home, and even when I'm alone just walking.

All Sofie and I did today was wave to each other while third and fourth graders played Marco Polo between us. After that, when she tried talking to me in the cafeteria I kept my face hidden behind my favorite *Magic Tree House* book. She said hi over and over until her smile went away. I just said "I can't talk right now" and pretended to care more about Jack and Annie living in the pages. Sofie left a rock on my porch today anyways to let me know that she's okay. The rock had dark brown stripes the same color as her skin. I put it in my pocket instead of around my bed with the rest of my collection.

What if Sofie and I never talk again? Maybe she will come to her senses and realize that I'm not really worth talking to anyways. Doesn't she know that I just ruin things? That I'll get her into trouble like her dad got into trouble. I don't know. I even had a dream about her waiting for me in the bathroom stall for confident walk practice, and I never showed up.

The truth is, I haven't stopped thinking about the valentine under Sofie's couch. Every morning I look at the drawing of it hanging next to my bed. I sometimes touch it to make it feel more real. One time Dad touched it too, and I hate it when he touches my personal property. He practically yelled with stinky breath, "Where did that drawing come from?" I kept my mouth shut, so instead he leaned in for a long time and kissed me good-night. I don't really remember what happened after that. Just that he took the *Magic Tree House* book out of my hands and said, "You'll get back to your old self in no time." I am still a boy, but I hate myself even more for being one. I'm sorry. I guess Dad never really did see me at all when he called me "his special girl."

I didn't want to tell anyone this, but I feel like I should. I'm not supposed to talk to college students or anybody who could give me any fancy "big-city attitudes." I'm sure I'm not supposed to be writing anybody this either. My parents found someone I'm supposed to tell everything to on Sundays instead. She had an ad in the yellow pages, but was also my grandpa's friend's friend. Mom says she is doing us a favor helping us like this. One of the first things the lady said to me was "You have such a pretty face." I'm supposed to say "Thank you" to that. She also wrote secret notes about me on a notepad I will never get to read.

On the way home after that, my mom noticed my frown all the way from the front seat. She turned around and said, "We're just doing what's best for you. Sometimes we know you better than you know yourself." I miss thinking that long car rides are for fun.

If you also went to the winter carnival this year, you would know that there was a big ice sculpture of the Wizard from *The Wizard of Oz*. It was humungous, almost the size of a house, and had THERE'S SNOW PLACE LIKE HOME carved into it. If I actually met a wizard like that, I would not ask him how to get back home. Would you? I would probably say something like "Do you know somewhere in the world where there are extra rooms and lemon trees in the wintertime?" That way, I could have a nice sleep and also Sofie and I can share a cup of lemonade again, and nobody will be in trouble.

None of this will last forever, right?

I'm sorry. I'll shut up now.

Sincerely,
I don't know

Friday, February 6, 1998

Hi.

Just wanted to say hi to someone today. I hope that's okay. I have to ask, do only Christmas trees have angels on top? Are angels in other places too?

Nathan Lucas had a cast on his arm today. He doesn't talk either, so he didn't say where it was from. I hope he's okay too. I hope he doesn't mind that I haven't signed it yet.

Sincerely, your friend,
Ellie Beck

Hi.

It's almost Valentine's Day. The holiday sure does make some people brave about their feelings. I'm not sure how brave I am feeling lately. Today I overheard Dylan Beaman say that he's going to go to the Sweetheart Skate Night with the Trampoline Lamda Kappa whatever Club for Valentine's Day this year. Courtney saw me staring, and told me to "Talk to the hand" when I wasn't even talking. I bet Dylan Beaman is going to hold hands with whoever looks the prettiest that night. They might even hug. I bet there will be an extra romantic slow skate, and they'll play that song "As Long as You Love Me" on the big speakers. I hate that Backstreet Boys song because it makes me want more than I could ever have.

Anyways, I promised myself I wouldn't talk about Sofie or the valentine she made me under her couch, so I won't. I won't talk about home. I won't talk about anything. It's whatever. Here's a drawing of a tornado in Kansas. I've never actually been there, but I feel like I have somehow.

I signed Nathan Lucas's cast
with the name Ellie, so I guess I
will here too. Hope you're okay.
I'm fine.

Ellie

Saturday, February 14, 1998

Hi,

I'm breaking a huge promise right now. I know that I'm not
supposed to think about Sofie, but I hope she knows that I

still care about her. I'm so sorry. I don't know what else to say about it. For the last two indoor recesses, she played alone with the light-up yo-yo she won from Jump Rope for Heart. She sometimes looked over at me, maybe hoping I would join. I just sat at my desk pretending to do my homework that's actually crumpled in the bottom of my backpack.

Really, I was just trying to figure out what valentine to give her. At this point, I've ripped out almost all of the paper from my math notebook trying to come up with the right thing to say.

Some of the letters I wrote just had gel pen scribbles between addition and subtraction problems. Some were hangman puzzles that I didn't actually know the answers to. I crumpled all of them. I don't know. Do you have any advice for writing a valentine that is nice, but definitely won't make anyone feel weird?

I could feel Dylan Beaman's eyes looking over as I was writing them. I already know he feels weird about me, so I just automatically balled up anything I didn't want him to see. I didn't want to risk him reading my feelings and telling them to the rest of the Trampoline Club that I still can't believe he's a part of. I feel kind of silly for saying this, but I actually thought about giving Dylan Beaman a homemade valentine too. I'm not sure why. It's not like he sits next to me every day because he wants to. I bet he would end up throwing it in the trash just like the Picture Day comb.

This needs to stay just between us, but I actually did write Dylan something like a valentine. It only took two commercial breaks of *Boy Meets World* to make. I have to admit, though, the letter will probably stay in the back of my notebook for forever because, even if I were a regular boy, I don't think Dylan like-likes boys. He would call any boy "gross" or something worse for wanting to hold his hand. He doesn't know that I'm a boy, though, which means I might still have a chance for him to like me.

The valentine I wrote for him just talks about how we're not that different at all, and that I wish he could see that. How would you feel if somebody gave you a letter like that? Especially if you thought the person who gave it to you was the weird girl in class with short hair? Secretly, I would love it if somebody wrote me a valentine that had those Backstreet Boys lyrics, "I don't care who you are, where you're from, what you did, as long as you love me."

Either way, it was way easier to write something for Dylan than it was for Sofie. I wound up filling the entire recycling bin with all my practice letters to her. The recycling bin sits quiet in the corner closest to the American flag, the little store where we can buy erasers, and the heavy classroom door. It's actually the size of a person scrunched up, but people walk past it all of the time. I bet none of them think about how many secrets it's filled with. Yesterday everyone lined up next to the bin wiggling and shouting ready to go home for the weekend. I think some of them just had too much sugar from their Valentine's Day candy. Sofie was at the back of the line reading *Harry Potter* for the third time, and Dylan Beaman was at the front of the line smiling to himself. I bet Dylan was busy thinking about showing off his hockey moves at the Sweetheart Skate. Maybe someone gave him one of those chalk-flavored candies that says BE MINE or CALL ME.

Nathan Lucas, that quiet boy, was so quiet that I didn't even realize he was behind me. His skinny arm reached out of the line and into the recycling bin. He picked up a notebook page from the top of the pile. I froze in place as he read the valentine. I hoped it was a hangman one, and nothing big like "Be Mine." I know deep down that I never should have thought the things that I have thought or wrote the things I wrote for Sofie, but it's not like Nathan Lucas knows who Rowan is anyways. Either way, I know he would never tell anyone about it. At recess, people make jokes that he wears short-shorts even though they all want to sign his new arm cast. He just plays with marbles alone. Nathan Lucas's face stayed straight, and he crumpled the valentine even more than before.

I watched him throw my letter back into the recycling bin a little bit wishing he knew that I was the one who wrote it. That way maybe we could play marbles together. I looked at him with big eyes as if I were asking him to be my new friend.

The last bell finally rang, and it might as well have been New Year's Eve for everyone else in my class. People probably would have thrown confetti if they had any. Even Nathan Lucas disappeared into the crowd of flying arms and legs. Not me. I was not excited to have another weekend of frozen feelings and one-person games of hangman. Mr. B walked the class out to the hallway like a parade. I would have bet on my life that nobody even noticed I that was not in line with them. I stayed behind to look into the deep blue recycling bin.

Sometimes I just feel really ready to just give up. People say that Yoopers would know how to survive World War III if there was one, but I'm not always so sure about myself. I wanted to hide inside of the recycling bin until the end of time. I don't ever want someone to think that I'm a crybaby. Everybody knows that boys aren't supposed to cry, but it could have been a relief to be in an ocean of my scribbles and all the things I have never said out loud. All of my crinkled-up papers inside would have been high enough to reach my knees. I know that I can't be the only person in class with secrets, but I have been feeling so alone and not even the quietest boy in class could figure it out when I looked at him.

You know when I mentioned those lyrics, "I don't care who you are, where you're from, what you did, as long as you love me"? Do you think anyone feels that way about me? Do you feel that way about me? I just don't know if I add anything good to anybody's life. I really wish I wasn't a boy. I wish I didn't like people in the wrong way. I heard on the news before that you can die from a disease for liking people in the wrong way.

I put one foot into the recycling bin, and felt the crush. I wondered if it would have been possible to drown in there, to get swallowed whole.

Suddenly, Sofie grabbed my wrist. She held on tighter than any of the twenty-something handholds we've ever had. I didn't even know that she stayed behind for me. She didn't have to especially since I didn't even give her a real valentine yet and I ignored her for characters in a chapter book. Heck, I tried to leave her behind when she has been having the hardest of times. She deserves much better than me. Before I could think another bad thing about myself, she cried out, "Rowan, you have to get out of there. The janitor could come and take you away forever."

I guess forever is a long time to be gone.

I'm trying my best to learn how to stay, and not get so lost in my scribbles. It just feels like I'll never know how to celebrate anything ever again, including the weekends. What kind of person can't even celebrate the weekends? I looked back into the pile of papers that filled the recycling bin, most of them were mine.

Sofie held on to my wrist until both of my feet were back safe on the ground. I wanted to say sorry for scaring her. I wanted to say sorry for being so far away and lying about being okay every time I put a rock on her porch. I didn't though. I didn't know how without making myself feel even stupider. She kept hold of my hand and said, "You are irreplaceable." She sounded kind of mad when she said that. I understand why she would be.

She opened the classroom door and I kept my eyes to the tile. I feel bad about saying this, but I still couldn't stop thinking about how good it would be to disappear.

It was the first time Sofie and I walked home together in a while. We were mostly quiet trying to avoid the black ice or maybe saying the wrong thing. I held my breath for half the time just praying that my parents didn't drive by and see us. The trees almost looked like empty hands reaching up to the sky without their leaves. Just about a block before Sofie and I went our own separate ways, she asked, "Is there anywhere you want to live when you become a grown-up?"

At first, I thought it was a silly question because I don't know any adults who I want to grow up to be like. Even so, Sofie said, "We're going to live for a long, long time, so we should think about it." I'm not so sure about that either, but she tried again by asking, "So what would our house look like?"

Don't you know she said *our* house, which means together. I hope that means that she forgives me. I closed my eyes trying really extra hard to imagine it, what a good home could be.

I told Sofie, "I would really love to live in a house on top of a big hill one day." I didn't mention this part to her, but high up is the best place to let go of balloons. I was thinking maybe Mont Ripley because there already are yellow chair-lifts and little wood sheds up there, or maybe something closer to where Richard lives, like Sugarloaf Mountain. Either way, Sofie pulled an empty carton of chocolate milk from her backpack and placed it on top of her black curls. She giggled as it sat perfectly between her pigtails.

She said, "That would be so great. We just have to find a milk carton big enough to fit you, me, my parents, and Viivi too." She laughed some more and said, "Until then, you can live in the carton on top of my head. I promise to give the best possible views of the playground." She spun around in a circle as if to show me the whole wide world. I will never ever forget that promise. One day, our house will have electricity, a playroom with stained-glass windows, and maybe a movie theater with red seats too.

I didn't want to stop thinking about this home together, but Sofie had to get back to her real home to help her mom babysit. She handed me the milk carton and said, "We'll be okay as long as we have our house." Then the two of us shook pinkie and decided it would be best if I kept it close for now.

The milk carton fit perfectly in the front of my brown overalls, but the views probably weren't as good as the top of Sofie's head. Mom must have seen it peeking out of my pocket, though. As soon as I got home, she told me that the carton needed to go in the trash. Instead, I went straight upstairs and hid it under my bed. I know that I buy chocolate milk almost every week at school, but this one was different.

But only an hour later, Mom peeked her head into my room and told me again, "That carton has got to go." I don't know why Mom suddenly cared so much about what happens in my room anyways. She went to bed early looking mad about it. Dad didn't come in my room to say good night either. He just stayed downstairs extra late with his shows. Having the carton made me feel safer than ever. I felt so good that I had a dream about flying over the playground. I was flying higher than the jungle gym and the maple tree, and I waved to everyone below. Some kids even smiled and waved back, including the ones who I never thought would.

At exactly seven o'clock this morning, Mom walked inside of my room again without knocking. I heard the door creek open, and watched her moose T-shirt between the light cracks of my quilt. I held my breath so still so that she wouldn't know that I was awake. Why do parents think that kids don't notice things? She was holding a noisy plastic bag from Kmart, and her white socks stepped right over my obstacle course of notebooks, rocks, and dirty laundry that I made around my bed.

She threw my milk carton in the bag, made a grossed-out noise, and walked away. I closed my eyes tight. All I could think about was how bad it would feel to tell Sofie what happened after we had just made up. Mom could have recycled it. That way, I could have at least dreamed about all the ways that milk carton could come back to me.

I'm sorry to say this, but at exactly eight o'clock, the garbage truck came to our house. It was green and the brakes squeaked super loud. I have never felt so sad looking out my bedroom window before. The garbage man threw the bags into the back of the truck with a bad clanky noise, like what was inside never mattered once. It mattered to me, but everybody decided it was just trash.

You know, I bet that garbage truck was full of things that other parents on my block didn't understand. Imagine how many valentines and milk cartons are in there. Landfills are supposed to be full of replaceable things, but I bet they're not. I've never actually been to the dump before, but I heard that the piles are bigger and taller than any houses I have ever seen. Even Canada brings their trash here. I don't know, I really wish I hid my milk carton better, just like everything else.

I have never said this out loud before, but I think Sofie is irreplaceable too. I hope I can find her a good valentine. In the meantime, I'm trying really, really hard to be okay and maybe turn in my homework on time.

Ellie

Thursday, February 19, 1998

Hi,

The recycling bin at school is now empty, it's as if nothing happened at all. I'm trying my very best to look on the bright side of things. For example, we got to play stuck in the muck in gym class. It's like a really fun version of tag where we all get to crawl under each other's legs like we're all friends. Our school also had a fire drill and everybody lived. Also, things aren't looking good for Cory and Topanga on the newest *Boy Meets World* because Cory asked for help from the wrong person. Then Topanga read a letter that she shouldn't have. I just hope they can work it out because they have been through so much together.

Anyways, I mostly just wanted to tell you that Dylan Beaman accidentally called me Rowan today. It was the closest he has come to talking to me in a long time. It was kind of nice even though I wasn't ready for the whole classroom to know that's my name. I accidentally dropped my SRT book in the hallway during our fire drill. When we finally got back to our seats, Mr. B asked the classroom, "Who does this belong to?" and held up my copy of *Magic Tree House: Ghost Town at Sundown*. Dylan Beaman knew I've been reading that and he shouted "It's Rowan's" without thinking at all.

Most people in the room didn't know who Dylan was talking about at first. They all looked right past me. I tried to make eye contact with Nathan Lucas to see if he at least remembered the name Rowan from my recycling bin letter. He kept on reading his book about some dragon instead.

I am Rowan, and I'm practically invisible to everyone who doesn't know that. I mean, have you ever had a whole room look right through you? It was so bad and there was nothing I could do about it. My face turned all white and Courtney pointed at me to say, "Oh my gosh, she looks like a ghost." Everybody laughed. She of all people knows that I'm not a ghost. At our old slumber parties, we talked to spirits with her Ouija board and nothing the magnet said was ever about me.

Mr. B walked over to my desk and placed the SRT book next to me with a small smile. I know he was trying to be nice, but I couldn't even look at him. He knows that I haven't been doing my homework assignments on time. I almost wanted to deny the whole thing and say "That isn't even mine," but lately all the teachers hang up paper cut-outs of dogs in the hallway every time we finish a book and I didn't want to lose that too. People in the hall will see I have enough paper dogs to pull a paper sleigh with the name Ellie Beck on it, and they will think I'm cool for reading so many books. They will forget about this whole day.

I wish Sofie was at school today when all of that happened, but she was absent. She probably had to babysit or maybe help her mom at her cleaning job. I just wanted to be real to somebody, for someone to look at me and understand. I looked back over to Nathan Lucas for one more chance, and again no luck. He was still reading. I guess I probably would have done the same thing if I were him. He has earned more paper cut-out dogs than anyone, and I bet his dad is proud of him. I pulled on my hangnail and I thought about pulling it the entire length of my body so I could have an excuse to go sit in the nurse's office. I didn't have the guts, though.

All of this might not sound like a big deal to you, but it was a big deal to me. Hopefully Sofie will be back in school soon and we can try doing our confident walks again.

This isn't a valentine, but I've been thinking a lot. I don't know who you are and maybe this is your first time finding one of my balloons, but you are important to me. Is there any chance you're in heaven? Are you a guardian angel? I've had lots of thoughts about who is reading all of my letters, but I don't know especially now that I don't go to church anymore.

Anyways, I should get going, but first you should know that you can try calling me Rowan even though it's a little bit scary for me. I don't know. Thanks for letting me change so much.

Sincerely,
Rowan Beck

Hi.

I found two quarters under the couch, so here I am writing another letter. I know that I'm not going to church with my family until I look good enough for people to see me, but sometimes I like to imagine that my balloon letters are going all the way up to God. Maybe it's possible even if Mom says that maybe God is too busy for us sometimes. I guess it just feels better not to pray in front of everyone else. I hope that's okay with you.

Anyways, lately people at school have been saying, "Girls rule and boys drool." Dad is a boy who drools. He reminded me last night with peanut M&M'S breath all over me. I don't know. To be honest, neither the boy or girl option is feeling very good right now. Aren't there other things to choose from? I know that I'm not supposed to ask so many questions, but the thing is that I don't like hunting or anything like that, and I don't like nail polish either. I just like what I like. Is that bad? If I were to pray enough, will I be good? Can I make this all go away and be like everyone else? I guess it's okay if you don't know the answer to that.

The lady I see on Sundays told my parents that I did a good job today. It's all because I let my mom choose my itchy outfit. I also didn't complain once when we pulled the car over to look at this memorial at a left behind copper mine. We have been there a million times, but Dad always likes to remind me it's where some girl named Ruth died because nobody was watching her close enough. People here say that the miners who died on the job died for our country, but I guess Ruth is different. I don't know. I think they're trying to teach me that only girls can get hurt.

A police officer with yellow-orange sunglasses was there at the memorial too. He just waved at us. I wonder if Ruth is safe now or if she is really still stuck in the lonely mine after all of these years, just like the plaque on the gate says.

I will say, I think it's true that boys can get hurt too. Maybe it just happens in a different way, like my dad's hand probably hurt after that time he hit his wall? Right? He was fighting himself, right? I don't know.

On the way home today, I told my parents I might become a hall monitor at school for having good grades and get chosen to go on the special safety patrol trip to the State Fair in Escanaba in August. I don't know why I said that because I haven't been good about homework and I don't even want to be a hall monitor. Even Dylan knows not to copy off of my papers these days. He has given up on me too. I guess I wanted Mom to be proud of me for what I could be. Dad gets prouder of me by the day, but it somehow doesn't feel right. I'm just feel really confused about things. I'm sorry.

Just so you know, I think I'm going to give up on sending this valentine to Sofie. It's just going to confuse everyone. Dad says, "Being bad is a choice, and it's up to you to learn how to shoot straight."

Are you glad I'm alive? Sorry if that's a hard question.

Hope you're okay.

Sincerely,
Ellie Beck

Tuesday, February 24, 1998

Dear You,

Things have been hard lately, so I'm just trying to hold on to the good stuff. If you don't mind me asking, do I really have to get rid of what I like in order for God to like me? Shouldn't others be happy when I'm happy? Today I felt like that could really be true when I put on my ice skates and I really felt close to the whole world. I spent more than half of the time skating backward, and I was really proud of myself. My very favorite part was Dad waving to me with a nice smile from the sidelines while I did "shoot the duck," where I bend down to hug my knees and somehow keep going. I felt big and I loved it. I felt big because my body was totally gone. I only remember touching the ice like it was a part of me.

Love is enough, right? Today, I feel like it is. Dad was even in a good mood on his ice skates too. He did a pretty twirl without showing off his hockey moves like every other dad does on the ice. Afterward, he gave me a high five and called me a name he hasn't called me in years, Sprout. I like it when he's like this.

Anyways, thanks for listening. I don't always share my wishes because I still think it's kind of bad luck, but I hope everyone at home can be in a good mood again tomorrow. I hope you're having a good day too.

Thanks,
Rowan Beck

Friday, February 27, 1998

Dear You,

If I had stickers, I would probably give myself a gold star today. I've had some new ideas, and I think they are ones worth keeping. It all started with Bill Nye the Science Guy. At school we all got to sit on the floor around the TV, and shouted the theme song "Bill, Bill, Bill, Bill, inertia is a property of matter" from the beginning. He talked all about bones and muscles, and why we need them so much using funny pancake examples. I haven't liked the human body unit in science class so much, but if I had to pick, this part has been my favorite.

Did you know that bones are actually pretty similar to rocks? It's so cool. Today I learned that humans are all born with three hundred bones, and we only have two hundred and six by the time we're grown-ups. It's because some bones come together when we grow and get stronger. Mr. B showed us using a plastic sheet on the overhead projector. I copied everything into my workbook and haven't stopped thinking about it since.

Today's lesson gave me the perfect idea for my valentine to Sofie. I am going to find her ninety-four rocks. I'll give her a rock for every bone that changes and gets stronger by joining other bones. I know I'm a few weeks late, but what do you think? I think she will love it. Plus, if anyone finds the valentine, they won't know the meaning just by looking at it, so it's safe. Either way, today was the perfect day to start digging for them because Sofie wasn't at school again.

I have to admit, Sofie has been missing a lot of school lately. She and her mom have been working extra hard because her dad can't do much to help from prison. On my way to recess, I quietly hummed "You Are My Sunshine" and thought of her. In my *ZooBook*, I learned that whale songs can travel up to ten thousand miles under the ocean. I imagined that Sofie could hear my song somehow too.

I started to dig around our usual recess spot at the giant rock. I don't have a rabbit's foot or anything like that, but I was in luck because the winter sun was actually strong enough to help break apart rocks and dirt still frozen together. I made a lot of progress while crawling along the bottom of the frosty slope. Within the first five minutes, I found three cool bumpy-lumpy rocks and a fourth one with glitter cooked into it. I put them inside of my front pocket, and they made a nice rattle every time I made a move. I felt unstoppable. It reminded me a little bit of my dad because he used to have a job where he dug all day for special rocks too. It was kind of nice to think about. After all, copper mines run in the family even though they're all rusted in the snow now.

But after a while, I looked down and noticed that my knees were all brown with cold, wet dirt. Mom would have had a cow if she saw that I already messed up my brand-new pants, especially because they're expensive and I have been growing fast. I then dug into my knees trying to make everything better and cleaner, but I found more and more dirt the harder I tried to wipe it off of me. I'm not sure how that happened. I somehow got a mess on my coat and my hands too.

It took a lot of focus and spit to dig the tiny brown specks out of my palms and nails. But then something covered up my light.

It was Dylan Beaman and the shadow of his body. He cleared his throat and said, "What are you doing?" He didn't even say it like it was a question. After all this time of not talking, you would think he could have come up with something nicer to say. Obviously Dylan hasn't been paying much attention in class if he didn't know that rocks are like bones, and they survive so much. I promise you that I did my very best to ignore him. I just tried to keep focus on getting the frozen dirt off my hands, digging into the long line closest to the top of my palm. I wasn't so sure why he was breaking the rules to talk to me anyways.

His shadow got even bigger and he said, "You move weird." I scratched into my skin a little bit deeper, trying to get every bad thing out of me. The pressure made every line in my hands turn red. Dylan Beaman really had a way of making me feel dirtier than the rocks.

Then he checked behind his shoulder, and said, "And your haircut looks like a big accident." I touched my hair, it's still way too short to hide into a ponytail. There was absolutely nothing that I could do to make myself better for him. It was just like that time on *Boy Meets World* when Cory messed up his hair and everyone laughed at him nonstop because he was so bad at middle school. Dylan wouldn't cut it out, and we aren't even in middle school yet. I couldn't believe it.

Then he repeated what he said about my haircut, as if I didn't hear him the first time. Don't you know, I've worked too hard to be called an accident. I bet the Trampoline Kappa Whatever Club told him to walk over to say all of those mean things to me. I spotted them all watching from the top of the wooden structure on the other side of the playground. I was too far away to read their lips, but Dylan came one step closer like he was going to crush me. It's no wonder I thought that he was inches taller than me for so long.

I tell you what, the first week of school now seems like forever ago. I remember back when Dylan shared his potato chips with me, back when he said I could be a part of something with all the other boys. People in class think he is so cool because he has light-up shoes, he knows a lot of fart jokes, and lately, he has been gelling his hair to look like a crashing wave. It turns out, he's not like me at all.

I didn't want to give him any more attention, but then he stomped his foot and the ice cracked. I could have been under that foot. I hate to admit this, but I could feel tears warming my cheeks. I was doing my best not to feel in front of him. I couldn't help it, though, and Dylan noticed. He called me a crybaby. It was time for me to be tough in a new way.

My short hair gave me nothing to hide behind. I stood up

and looked at Dylan right in the eyes. It's something I have never done with a crush. I felt his size in that moment.

Our eyes might be the same color, but mine were full of tears and Dylan's looked empty. I didn't take mine off of his for a second. I no longer wondered if he was afraid of the big snake in the science room. I no longer wondered what his favorite songs were for dancing silly, and what he thought of his uncles and aunts. I no longer wondered about what he does when he's alone. He has probably never wondered anything about me.

I balled my left fist and used my right to point him in the other direction.

Surprisingly, Dylan actually turned around to leave when I did that. He walked across the white field, back toward the structure. It wasn't until then I saw he also had a dirt stain on the back of his light blue jeans. I don't really understand Dylan Beaman at all. I have decided that I'm done with crushes and people who make me want to hide my dirty hands and knees. I would rather dig for someone who will really remember me. In fact, I found six more good rocks at recess today that are all worthy of being valentines. Dylan Beaman won't get any of them, not one. They are for Sofie.

I am sick of people telling me I am bad when I feel good and telling me I am good when I feel bad. I am sick of people with their own dirt stains telling me about mine. I'm so mad, and that's fine. I have a lot more rocks to dig for, eighty-four to be exact. I would say that you can come and help, but I want to do this on my own. Thanks for listening.

Sincerely,
Rowan, that's my name don't wear it out

Saturday, March 14, 1998

To Whoever Is Reading This,

Instead of getting a balloon last week, I used my allowance money to make four wishes into the Pilgrim River. All of my quarters sank straight to the bottom and I could see my wishes shine between the rocks below. Maybe that means something good will happen soon.

I was feeling so strong the last time I wrote balloon mail, but I have been feeling confused about what to write down since then. I don't want to get into trouble. I'm afraid whoever reads this is going to think I'm bad or tell on me. I'm afraid that you'll see my life and decide that I'm just a crazy person that needs to get fixed or go away forever. I'm afraid

you'll be like everybody else, but I'd like to try sharing anyways if that's okay with you.

Just so you know, I gave Sofie her valentine. Believe it
or not, the ninety-four rocks I dug up were so heavy that I
had to walk to her house almost every day this week to get
the whole entire present to her. Like usual, it was so quiet
at Sofie's house without Richard there singing or walking
in with a plate of coffee cake. Whenever I opened my backpack to empty out the rocks, they were the loudest thing in
the house. They knocked on her wood floor like they were
excited to finally be home.

My favorite rock I found for Sofie was an almost green
color, like the ones you can mine copper from. I think it was
even more beautiful than fool's gold. I scooped it up from
the bottom of the river after I made my wishes. I dried it off
with my fuzzy sweater and made another wish on it. I kept
it safe in my secret backpack pocket, so I could give her the
special rock at the very end. Sofie's eyes twinkled when I
put it in her hands. She balled up her fist with the rock safe
inside, and she hugged me just as tight. She told me thank
you a million times and said, "I promise I'll find a perfect
place to put all these little treasures." She called them treasures, and I think she really meant it.

It felt good to share, but I was feeling really weird after our
long hug. I'm not sure how to describe it. I crossed my arms
and practically whispered, "Promise not to tell anyone I

called the rocks a valentine?" I didn't want her or anyone else to get the wrong idea. I don't know. She agreed with me anyways. She said a little louder than me, "Sure, it's not a valentine. I don't even want it to be one." I know I'm the one who said it first, but I had to go into the hallway to cry. I lied to her and said "I have to go to the bathroom now."

I didn't do anything wrong giving her a valentine, right? It's not like anything really happened. Either way, I was kind of afraid to go to the Friday Fish Fry with my family after all of that because they all still think Sofie is a bad influence. My shoulders slouched over my steamy plate. Dad tried to be nice by getting me a Mackinac fudge sundae, but it didn't help. My backbones felt heavy with all the weight of those rocks, with the weight of a lot of things I'm not even sure how to say. Do you ever feel like you're still carrying something even if it was from a while ago? I don't know.

I used to be so good at imagining the places I wanted to explore and the parts of myself I really wanted to be, but lately it has felt hard to do that. When I look at the tree, I decide it is just a tree. When I look at the birds, I don't care about their wings. I even turned in an empty test at school this week. I'm not usually like that. Even something simple, like looking at myself in the hallway mirror this morning, made me feel so far away.

Last Friday, Courtney made fun of the way that I held Sofie when we went down the slide together. I thought we were being brave letting everybody see, but Courtney said, "You can't hold Sofie like that if you're not a boy." She squinted her eyes at me hard as if she couldn't see me there. I haven't been able to hear anything else since, not even birds or the swish-swish of my own windbreaker.

My parents took me on another long car ride this week-end too. For the hundredth time, Dad passed that empty mine where that girl Ruth died. He shook his head and said again, "That girl didn't know what she was doing. Someone could have kept her from getting hurt." I know we have been doing this thing every Sunday for a while now, but I didn't want one more person calling me a confused girl. That's not how you think of me, right? If anything, I'm a confused boy, or just a really tired one. So many of the trees we passed on the highway still looked dead to me.

Dad turned up the radio and we had to listen to that "I'll be your crying shoulder" song. I caught him looking at me through the rear-view mirror and felt like everything that God let go of and dropped on the ground. Is there something I'm supposed to learn in all of this, other than how to be a girl that my family can love? I'm just not so sure what everyone wants from me. Girls aren't the only people who get hurt, right?

When we eventually pulled up to the doctor's office, I pressed the red buckle only halfway and pretended my seat belt was stuck on. I wanted to be left behind, but they wouldn't let me. My mom pulled me out by saying "I love you" over and over again. Maybe she does love me, but I don't know. What if I think about God in a different way than everyone else? Do you ever feel like you don't have any choices? Have you ever messed up while giving someone a valentine?

I don't know what else to say. I used my very last quarter to wish for school to be better, but I guess wishes are like prayers and they can take a while to come true. I don't know. I'm just not so sure how long I can wait.

Anyways, I'm going to go now. Sorry.

> Sincerely,
> I don't know, sorry

Sunday, March 15, 1998

Hi.

Today I just wanted it to be spring, but Michigan lives under a cloud most of the time. I was tricked into thinking that it would be warm outside because the ground smelled like earthworms and the sun was peeking out. I threw on my windbreaker and told my parents I was going to the lake all by myself.

The truth is that I stopped at Sofie's house first, and the weather changed completely by the time I got to her driveway. I had to zip up one of the million zippers all the way to my chin, but there really was no place to hide from the extra cold wind. I hugged myself a little tighter, and squeezed my eyes shut wishing that my windbreaker had a hood. If any other Yooper this far north saw me like that, they would have called me a "buck, buck, buck, chicken" for not taking the cold with a straight face. I couldn't help it, though. The sky was howling and it almost felt like the Earth was trying to erase me, and I was disappearing fast.

I don't know how long I waited for Sofie, but she was wearing the biggest frown ever when she finally came outside. You should have seen it. She just stood in the doorway and stared at the dusty driveway for a whole minute. She later told me that she was just imagining Richard pulling up in the carriage car. Sometimes I wish I could do more. Sofie covered her eyes with her blue hood and put her feet just a few inches from mine.

I asked, "Can we go walk for the longest time?" Sofie nodded, but it took a while for her to finally uncover her watery eyes. Sofie and I might as well have been in two separate worlds walking all those minutes in silence. Even the sun took a break as we stepped heavy on the cracks because we didn't care about our luck at all. The good news is that the farther we walked away from our neighborhood, the fewer cracks there were to step on. The cement sidewalks went away completely and there were only paths of the tiniest rocks into the woods.

After we passed the NO TRESPASSING signs, empty-looking houses, and yellow quilt store, Sofie's face started to come alive. Her eyes were full of questions and specks of amber again. We were now far enough from home to finally see the lake horizon through the skinny tree trunks. The wind blew at its fullest, pushing us closer to the water. The birds made shadows flying above the surrounding tall grass. Maybe they were all telling us to keep going too. I bet they were. The sound was like an invisible orchestra, the sound that clouds make when I let go of a bunch of balloons.

We walked and walked until we reached a tiny patch of sand with left behind canoes. Somehow sand got into Sofie's Skechers. We paused to shake them out, the wind carried away the golden dust before any of it could fall onto the ground. She held my shoulder to put her shoes back on and I wiggled and waved to keep balance. Our silence turned into laughs that couldn't help but just fall out because there was nobody but the birds to watch us.

We traced each other's shoe prints below the seagulls singing with their whole voices. They soared so high I never thought that they could come down. Then out of the blue, one of them landed right in front of us with a small plop. He fluffed his gray feathers and turned his little head to the side.

We didn't have fries or anything like that to offer, but he still hopped a little closer, like he remembered us from somewhere. I do wish that seagull stayed longer, but it seemed like he had another place to be. Sofie and I waved goodbye as we watched him go off with all the other excited birds. He didn't seem to think twice about where his friends were, and they all flew away toward Dollar Bay together. I kept on waving goodbye even when they were gone.

Sofie laughed again. I said, "What's so funny?" She told me, "Your arms make the same swish-swish sound as the seagulls."

Today, I really don't care if you reading this are God or the universe, or a nice person, a tree branch, or a bird reading this letter. I'm realizing that it's all kind of the same to me. Whenever Sofie and I are just walking together, I can imagine again. Is there anything in this world that helps you imagine again? Even when everything else makes it feel just impossible?

I love you,
Rowan


PS, I'm actually sending this balloon to you on Tuesday, March 17. Nothing so big has happened these past few days other than finding a Twix bar on the cafeteria floor, and also Mom buying me a new smiley-face headband. My half-birthday happened too, but that doesn't mean much. To be honest, I wasn't so sure about how I ended my letter to you, especially because I don't even check under the WELCOME TO HOUGHTON sign anymore. I didn't even mean to say "I love you." It just kind of slipped out and I wasn't thinking. I'm sorry.

I'm not even totally sure what love means anyways. So, I can take it back if you want me to or if it made you feel weird. I'm really sorry about that.

Sincerely,
Rowan

Sunday, March 22, 1998

Hi,

I'm not sure if you've been watching *Boy Meets World* these days, but either way, you should know that Cory and Topanga officially broke up. Cory really isn't taking it well. Everybody tells him he's too depressing to be around, and he doesn't want to be around himself either. He and his best friend went to a party and got as sloppy as my dad, and then they even got detention. I think I understand how Cory feels. This weekend was so good and so bad at the same time, but I don't want to be depressing to be around either. I don't know. I think that I only want to tell the good parts, if that's okay with you.

The good part of my weekend all started yesterday when I went to Sofie's for a slumber party, even though I told my parents I was at Courtney's house. Don't worry too much about that, though.

Anyways, the first thing Sofie and I did was tuck in her baby sister. It was kind of like a chore, but it was fun too. We turned on Viivi's lullaby tape with my old Rapunzel Barbie by her side, and she magically stayed sound asleep the whole night. Sofie and I tiptoed out of her room, and then gave each other the world's quietest high five.

After that, we hopped down the stairs to the basement, where the real slumber party started. We could make as much noise as we wanted down there. Sofie played an awesome drum solo on the already wobbly railing. It almost sounded like that "we will, we will rock you" song that the paper football players sing during the biggest games. I tried to add another cool beat to Sofie's song with my feet, and threw all of my things down the stairs for the grand finale.

I love basements. It's so cool to have an entire floor that even the smartest people can't see from the outside. Some say that basements were invented to protect families and cans of food from getting hurt in big storms. When a tornado comes, the weatherman always calls basements "shelter." Have you ever seen a tornado in real life before? I haven't, but I know a little bit about them and what happens to the dirt, rocks, and broken houses that all get lost in the middle part.

All I can say is that I sure did feel safe in Sofie's basement. She actually made it as safe as possible by making a fort ahead of time with two chairs and five blankets. It even had its own living room, kitchen, and bedroom. I never thought my dream house would be so small, but life can be surprising like that.

Sofie actually hasn't been over to my house since that one night we made our maps to the moon. It's okay, though. Her house is better than mine. Plus, Mrs. Gavia left out a real-meat meatloaf, plus red pop, three bowls of snacks, and a whole bunch of craft supplies. I have gotten so used to playing house with invisible spaghetti and donuts, so it was like a miracle to see real, good-smelling food sitting in our fort's kitchen. I know it sounds silly, but I almost didn't want to touch it, like everything would somehow disappear if I got too close. Sofie didn't think twice and took the first handful of pretzel sticks. Then she took a second handful, and I took the third.

After that, Sofie and I did some confident walk practice, but then we did something completely different and cut out lots of construction paper. The pieces of paper got smaller and smaller, the size of little square ants. Her cat Dusty loved watching that part, and pawed at our growing piles until she fell asleep. Sofie and I must have made a million pieces, and we sang with the Spice Girls, "I'll tell you what I want, what I really, really want" louder than anything. Dusty's ears perked up and she bolted upstairs, and it was so funny. We were probably ten times louder than any winter concert solo. I actually can't remember the last time I let myself be that noisy, let alone shout about what I really, really want.

We turned off all the lights and counted down, "five, four, three, two, one," and screamed, "ZIGAZIG AHHH." We picked up our rainbow confetti by the handful and threw it as high as we could. My arms stretched out all the way into the pitch black and I could feel the pieces moving all around me. Sofie tapped on my shoulder with "I have an idea." I love it when she says that. She fumbled through the dark and plugged in every night-light one by one. The lights circled the whole room like a family of fireflies, their yellow glow brightened all the places we couldn't see before. We quickly discovered a bunch of our confetti landed on top of the fort blankets, in our hair. Some fell perfectly into the back my sweatshirt. I pulled my hood up, and let the colorful pieces slowly fall in front of my eyes.

We played another game after that. I showed Sofie how to make crowns using needle, thread, and popcorn. It felt good to teach something I know I'm good at. I pulled the sewing needle through each little kernel without trying hard at all. Sofie followed my lead, and she was a real natural at it. The butter actually made the jewelry look like it was made out of gold. Tying the knot at the end is always the hardest part, though, because everything can come undone just like that. Luckily, Sofie offered me her hand. I wrapped the string tight around her finger and then looped the two ends so they can never come apart. I think that's what the song "2 Become 1" is all about.

Anyways, Sofie and I put the pretty popcorn crowns on each other's heads. I hoped that we would smell like movie theater butter forever and ever. After that, we made up a long secret handshake that involved doing a bow and curtsy for each other. We smiled and smiled until we accidentally pointed at each other's crowns and said "You did a great job" at the same exact time. It was so funny that we forgot to call jinx. It really felt like we were glowing in the dark while we giggled about nothing. We had to lie down and put hands on our bellies to make our laughing stop.

Then out of the blue, Sofie rolled over and her smile changed. She took a big bite of leftover popcorn and looked at me. I got nervous that maybe I had done something wrong, like maybe she noticed that I did a bow instead of a curtsy. But then she asked, "Truth or truth?" Of course I said "Truth."

"Tell me one of your biggest secrets," she practically dared me.

I know I said that I wouldn't share anything bad in this letter, but I have to tell you something.

I didn't tell the truth at all for that "truth." I ruined the game, and told her someone else's secret instead. I told Sofie about the girl who always sits at the lunch table behind me. She was actually born sick with something. I forget what it's called, but it makes it hard to ride a bike. There are just some things that I can't tell Sofie yet. Do you think something is a secret when I can hardly say it to myself? I don't know.

Do you think I was born sick? I know that God didn't make a mistake in making me a girl, but I know who I am and I know I'm much more than my body. God doesn't even have a body. I know that my parents feel differently. They are trying to fix me.

Mom and Dad actually hate my haircut so much that last weekend they made me wear a flower hat when I was outside at the same time as the neighbors. They want people to know what I'm supposed to be. My parents don't even want me at church because they don't want anybody to ask questions about me. Please don't tell anyone that I'm not allowed to go to church anymore. A lot of kids at my school are getting their reconciliations right now. I'm not so sure what it actually means, but I feel like I'm supposed to get a reconciliation too. I wish I could tell Sofie all of this, but I can't. I don't want Sofie to worry about me, and there's nothing she can do to stop it anyways.

Mr. B always likes to say "We are as sick as our secrets," and I think finally I get what that means now.

Sorry if this is too much. I almost just want to stop writing and send my balloon now, so I don't have to look at this anymore. This is exactly why I didn't tell Sofie the truth about Sundays when she asked me about my big secrets. There are a lot of other things I could have told her too, about my parents, about my dad. But I can't go there. It's too much, and maybe I am too.

So, you know what I did after that? I told Sofie more lies, one about a time we saw Bigfoot at Girl Scout camp, another about Jax the dog coming over to my house. She listened that whole entire time with her mouth open, like she was trying to take in every word I said. I love that she always believes in me, but I kind of wish she didn't that time. Don't you know I was just trying to be normal and go to a regular slumber party and feel good. I really don't know how to do that, though.

I didn't want to talk anymore after that.

I asked her, "Can we go sit in our old ship now?" She nodded, and we climbed inside of the refrigerator box. I noticed she has been drawing all kinds of pictures on the cardboard sides, rainbows even. It felt a little bit smaller than before, so Sofie and I had to curl up into a ball together. We both smelled like popcorn. Sofie's long dark hair blended with mine, and her hand was only inches away. I closed my eyes and started to dream of our box floating down a river together. I don't know how long we were there for, but I knew deep down that we couldn't just fall asleep together like that.

I took away my hands to rub my eyes and fake a yawn. We crawled out of the ship and into our own sleeping bags. Both of our heads fit perfectly under the two kitchen chairs holding up our fort. We said our quick good-nights, but I couldn't fall asleep. I wasn't sure where I was allowed to look, so I just stared at the tree rings underneath the chair for what felt like an hour.

Maybe it was two in the morning at this point, but I eventually rolled onto my side to try emptying out my brain. My thoughts usually get the loudest at nighttime. Sofie was just close enough for me to hear her breathing slow and steady with a tiny yawn in between. I stayed as still as I could until my breathing matched hers.

Is it weird to call someone beautiful when all the lights are off, and we can't even see each other? I went to sleep instead of finding out.

That night I dreamt I was in a shipwreck with my dad. He lived, but I fell into the sea. I sank and sank just when I thought water was for floating. They say that if you die in your dream, you die in real life, but I woke up extra early this morning with crust in my eyelids and a burning lump in my throat. Maybe it was my punishment for something.

I inched my knees as close to Sofie as possible without touching. She had her worn princess sleeping bag pulled all the way up to her eyes. I whispered, "See you tomorrow at school, I hope." I knelt next to her waiting for her to say something back, but she didn't wake up. That felt like the wrong way to say goodbye, but I had to get home and put a purple headband in my hair before my parents came back from church. I knew that we were going on another long drive today. I crawled out of our fort, and stumbled in the dark to put everything into my backpack.

When I got upstairs, I was surprised to see Mrs. Gavia in the kitchen wearing her striped pajamas and hairnet. She looked almost as tired as me, except she is allowed to drink coffee. She was putting Viivi in the high chair and she asked me, "Don't you want anything to eat?" I was just trying to leave without anybody noticing, so I stood there like a deer in headlights. I couldn't think of a good escape plan, so I said in a scratchy voice "Yes, thank you" to the easiest thing possible.

She dug through the kitchen cupboards and asked me two times in a row, "Are you okay going home, honey?" That's when I started a new round of the no talking game. I'm still playing, and not just because I have a sore throat.

I ended up leaving Sofie's house with a bunch of corn cereal in my hands and a little bit in my windbreaker pockets too. It tasted like the healthiest thing I've ever had in my whole life, much healthier than my usual Cookie Crisp and buttery toast. I have to admit, I didn't know what to think of it. Hopefully Mrs. Gavia never finds out, but I decided to feed the little cereal pieces to some happy-looking tree rats and keep walking.

The rest of that walk felt lonelier than most. The sun was so bright outside, I had to squint my eyes. There were no clouds to give pretty silver linings. The trees didn't have shade either because they're still trying to make new leaves. I don't know what in the world those trees are waiting for. I could feel the heat from my throat spread into a fever and the sides of my head started knocking when I realized I left my popcorn crown in Sofie's basement. I think I forgot my toothbrush too. I can't believe I did that.

I actually thought about just walking forever and skipping this entire day, but I didn't. You know what stopped me? I wanted to write this letter first. I wanted to tell you about all the good parts so then I could remember them better. I hate thinking that I was born sick, and that everybody thinks Sofie is somehow making it worse.

I know that we're strangers and all, but just promise that you won't try to fix me, okay? I'm only sick with a cold or something.

Sincerely,

Me

Hi again,

What do you think about the phrase "Dance like nobody is watching"? It's written on a piece of fake wood in our living room. Mom loves inspiring words like that. The thing is, though, I've never actually seen her dance before. Maybe she only does it when nobody is watching. Do you ever let people watch you with their eyes or with their camcorders?

I secretly like to dance. When I let myself move, I really jump, I really leap. One time in Sofie's basement, we pretended we were the Spice Girls at the Mr. Steps dancing boot camp. We wiggled around with umbrellas and leaped over inflatable lake tubes, just like in the movie *Spice World*. After that, we listened to Sofie's Selena tape, and she showed me this cool dance move called the washing machine. It's like the Macarena, but all in your hips. It wasn't like gym class, which makes me feel like anything I do with my arms and legs is so wrong. Especially when we had our square dancing unit, I really hated that.

Gym is actually the worst and it's the only class that doesn't have inspirational quotes on the walls. If I were in charge, I would change that. Gym class today was especially tough. There was no jungle gym obstacle course or play parachute or anything fun like that. Nathan Lucas led us through ten jumping jacks, ten crunches, and ten toe touches with his one arm free because the other one is still in a cast. After that, the gym teacher made two students be team captains for the day. The captains stood in front of the whole room and picked people one by one to join their teams. And you know what? I hate that because they always choose their friends, so I always get picked close to last. You're very lucky if you have never had this problem.

Of course Dylan was one of the two captains this afternoon. He wanted to make the perfect baseball team. I honestly don't know why we bothered, because Yoopers aren't even supposed to play baseball. It's just supposed to be hockey, basketball, football, maybe soccer, and then more hockey. I guess I'm not so good at any of those either. I waited for five whole minutes until there was just me and Nathan Lucas waiting to get picked. Maybe it's cool to be left with the stretch leader of the day, but I could tell Dylan was doing "eeny, meeny, miny, moe" to decide who to pick between the two of us. Nathan Lucas jingled the marbles in his pockets, and kept his eyes on his bruised knees.

Dylan finally pointed at me and said, "You, I guess." Even though I won, I felt like a real leftover. I couldn't help but wonder if he was going to try to step on me again. Having my own captain not want me there made me not want to try at all. I wish Sofie had been there. I know that it's not really her fault for needing to babysit Viivi while her mom is working, but I was feeling pretty mad that she couldn't be at school again. Why does she have to get punished just because of something Richard did? It's not even really his fault either. I don't even know who to be mad at. Sorry, I'm sorry. Anyways, the whole class went to the field outside. The ground was still wet from the storm last night. It even smelled like rain.

Do you ever know that something is going to be really bad even before it starts? Mary decided it was a good idea to pick up an earthworm and show it off to Dylan. I hated watching the pink guy wiggle and get scared like that. Mary used to think zoos were animal jails, and now she doesn't care about anybody but Dylan and the new goldfish she won at a PTO fundraiser. It was one of the only times in my whole life that I didn't mind the gym teacher blowing her whistle all loud like that. Mary threw the worm and put her hands behind her back. The gym teacher shouted "Cut the horseplay" and handed an orange plastic bat to the first kid.

Everybody on Team Dylan stood around watching the field like it was a big stage, and I ended up being second in line to bat. I never would have done that on purpose. The whole class seeing me try to hit the ball has always been one of my least favorite things about springtime. I was so nervous about my turn that I tried to find something to do with my hands. That didn't work out so great because I accidentally pulled the drawstring of my navy blue shorts way too far. The string nearly came out completely, and I had to wiggle my fingers over the fabric to make it better.

That's when Mary leaned in to Dylan's ear to say, "Why are Ellie's legs so hairy?" Of course I could hear her saying something bad about me with the wrong name. It was such a loud whisper. Dylan repeated her question even louder. It made me think of one time when the Sunday doctor asked me, "What are the other girls in your class doing?" when she was looking at my legs. Please don't tell anyone this, but I kind of want my leg hair to stay forever. It's easy to forget that, though, with Mary and Dylan laughing like that.

I kicked the closest dandelion and held my breath, and tried wishing for something so big that I couldn't even think of anything. The white seeds traveled across the bases, toward the blacktop where they might not ever grow. My leg hair is long and soft and seemed to cover everywhere when I looked down. I tried to cover it all with my hands, but it wasn't nearly enough. The gym teacher then shouted "Ellie, up" in a way that made even more people look at me. I dragged my feet over the dandelions on my walk to the field. Maybe it was cheating trying to get that many wishes at once.

I picked up the plastic bat. It felt empty on the inside. I hated holding it because it suddenly left my legs with nothing to cover them. I hated it so much that it was hard to breathe. I let the first two baseballs fly right past me. On the third try, I surprised myself and hit the ball. It landed in the grass a few feet away with a big plop.

I was the first kid in class to get a hit, but no one clapped for me. Everybody just stared some more. I accidentally threw the bat too far and then ran around like a penguin, keeping my arms straight to my sides. All I cared about was trying to cover my legs. That sure made it hard to play the game right, and I got out before I even made it to first base. The whole entire class watched me like they already knew it would happen, and less than first base was exactly what they were expecting.

I hope you're reading this not thinking I'm a doofus or, even worse, a doofus with bad, hairy legs. Maybe I'll fail gym class too. I went to the back of the batter line pretending like nothing ever happened. I am bad at pretending, though. I need to work on that too. I kept my hands tight over my knees and stared at the last white dandelion in sight. If it hadn't been so far away, I would have wished that there would be no more running for the rest of the day.

Team Dylan did end up winning today's baseball game, but it obviously wasn't because of me. When we lined up to go back inside, Nathan Lucas surprised me by asking, "Was there any math homework due today?" It was our first conversation ever, and it will probably be our last. Dylan Beaman noticed us and said, "Don't ask her. She doesn't talk anymore." I couldn't say anything to that, of course. So I just shook my head, hopefully with the right answer. I bet Nathan Lucas doesn't like me now because nobody said anything at all after that. I admit, I miss the old Dylan. Maybe he was just trying to get another boy to join the Trampoline Club. I think he's the only boy in it right now. I just wish he would ask me.

Can I be honest with you? I sometimes feel like I'm running out of places to go. I know Mr. B would probably say right now to forget about "Dance like nobody is watching." Instead, we are supposed to "Dance like someone who loves you is watching." I know for a fact that my mom would never hang a sign that said that in the living room.

If I could have a new wish right now, it would be for more people in my life who want to watch me no matter what. That would be kind of like having built-in teammates, the kind with matching shirts and knee scrapes. Good teammates would say something like "Your leg hairs are like a forest, but not the kind of forest to hide in." If I become a teacher one day, I would make an inspirational poster that says something like that. I would hang it next to the water fountain, inside the bathroom stall, or other places people go to be by themselves. I know my parents think I should join the army when I grow up because I have a weird haircut and it's a reliable job, but maybe I really could be a teacher.

What do you think? My grades aren't the best right now, but I still think it could be a good thing.

I have to say, I wouldn't ever want to grow up to be a gym teacher, but I kind of wish that Mr. B was ours. He would never make us all run relays or fifty-meter dash competitions, and he definitely wouldn't use a whistle either. Sometimes he even draws smiley faces next to the name Rowan on my school papers, even if he doesn't call me that out loud.

Anyways, I'm going to try to do some of my homework now. I hope you're okay, wherever you are.

Sincerely,
Rowan Beck


PS, So, the Kids' Choice Awards will be on TV this Saturday. I'm only telling you this because it might be the last year I get to watch it because that's just not what you're supposed to do once you're in middle school. Last year Rosie O'Donnell got slimed, and maybe it will happen again. Do you think Rosie has leg hair too? I hope so. Why do people have leg hair anyway? Everyone has it, so is it weird if I like mine? Sorry if I already asked you that, I'm just thinking about stuff.

Sincerely again,
Rowan Beck

Hi,

I watched the Kids' Choice Awards tonight when my dad went out to that bar, Dave's, but he actually brought Mom with him this time. The point is, I got some peace and quiet to watch my show. You might think I'm too old for Nickelodeon now, but it was actually really great. First of all, that Puff Daddy performed a song called "I'm Coming Out" before he got slimed, and all of the grown-ups kept saying "Kids rule" over and over again. Rosie O'Donnell said it the most and she was in charge of the whole awards show. She also popped a balloon, and nothing bad happened. She smiled and laughed when it blew up in her face. I've never been that happy when my mail balloons popped. But I really like her.

Anyways, a few people thanked God on stage when they got their blimp awards. When Sabrina the Teenage Witch won, she actually thanked her family. Will Smith even offered to get his mom a sandwich in his speech. I'm not sure why, but I can't stop thinking about that. I wonder what it's like to thank your family for something and really mean it. I hope it's something I can do one day. For now, I'm just hoping Dad will go to sleep really fast tonight. I'm starting to think that maybe kids aren't supposed to be treated like the way I get treated sometimes. Do you know what I mean? Anyways, I'm going to try going to bed now.

Rowan

Thursday, April 9, 1998

To Whoever Reads This,

Gosh, I wish I actually talked to Sofie on all of those days I was too quiet for my own good. She wasn't at school again today. I watched her empty chair for the entire "Pledge of Allegiance" instead of the flag. If I could, I would do anything to help. I would wash windows with Sofie and her mom, read Viivi *A Very Quiet Cricket* until the pages chirp at the end. I know deep down it's not Sofie's fault, but, holy moly, why can't she be here? We are getting so behind on our confident walk practice and I bet she's getting behind on her homework too.

I missed Sofie even more at recess. I'm kind of embarrassed to say this, but I brought my MTV binder with me to recess again in case people still thought it was cool. I can tell you now that it didn't help me at all. I sat under the jungle gym that's shaped like a giant bubble, and watched my classmates through the gaps. Almost everyone in my grade was playing soccer on the hill with Michigan versus Michigan State teams. The boys all ran up and down the yellow grass shouting each other's names, calling "I'm open, I'm open," while the girls trotted along the sides and talked. I wondered if any of the girls actually wanted to play more. Either way, I felt so far away watching all of them. I might as well have been watching TV too tired to change the channel.

Gina gave up on the soccer game halfway through, and ran toward the jungle gym. I actually heard a rumor that she is the first girl in our class to get her "thing at the end of the sentence." That means Gina is going to be cool forever because every girl wants to ask her questions about what it's like to be a real woman and never watch the Kids' Choice Awards again. I didn't think to ask her about any of that at recess today. She jumped up on the jungle gym. I was surprised to see her pink fingernails so close to me. I couldn't tell from her dark mood ring if she was happy to see me, but she moved up the bars quick and flipped her whole body upside down. Gina's hair dangled down, her brown eyes opened wide. I could see shades of green and blotches of blue that I had never noticed before. Our eye contact right there was probably the longest five Mississippi seconds of my whole life.

It stopped all of a sudden when the soccer ball came flying toward us. Dylan chased after it, and Gina turned rightside up for him. She right away pointed at my haircut and called me a bad word that she probably learned from her professor dad or maybe even a college student. I'm not sure what it meant, but I know it was bad because Dylan Beaman smiled in a way that I knew. I think Gina only said those things because he was standing there. In an alternate universe, maybe she and I could have become friends again if it wasn't for Dylan's interrupting. Maybe Gina and I would have made plans to get wristbands at the Houghton County Fair or promised to stay up all night waiting for her lava lamp to move. Maybe she would have told me in the dark what it's like to have a period and use Teen Spirit deodorant. I don't know.

Dylan kicked the ball back to his Michigan State team and joined Gina on top of the jungle gym instead. The two of them didn't look down at all, but their legs went through the bubble right above my head. I don't think I could have even stood up without getting kicked. That's when Gina kept going on and on about the bad word that I am. She even said, "Ellie's kind of like the purple Teletubby." I've never even seen that show, so how am I supposed to know what that means. I'm starting to think that I watch all the wrong TV channels. I pressed my feet deeper into the sand, my arms tighter around my legs, praying just to be normal again. I bet people wouldn't have cared this much if I called Dylan cute last summer. I'm really embarrassed to say this, but I still sometimes think about wanting to hold his hand and I know I shouldn't.

I just stayed in the sandy bottom all recess long waiting for something to change. I tucked my legs all the way inside of my sweatshirt and pulled up my hood to hide my growing haircut. I held myself, like a hug, like the caterpillar's cocoon that used to hang in the jungle gym. I wonder what caterpillars do in there all day anyways. I bet they are really good at listening because what else could they even to do in there? I don't know, I change most when I'm listening too.

When the recess bell finally rang, I listened to all the other kids run past me, laughing, screaming. I stayed balled in my sweatshirt until they all lined up to go back inside. Nathan Lucas was the only one to notice me there in the bubble. He touched the bar with dirty fingernails, and looked at me for a few seconds. I kind of wanted to say something, but he walked away when the recess aid's whistle blew for the second time. Nathan Lucas has been looking over at me a lot lately. I don't know what to think about it, but I hope he doesn't hurt me. Maybe I shouldn't have said that.

I'm sorry. Thank you for reading this far if you have read this far, but I don't really want to bother anybody with anything. I didn't even put a rock on Sofie's porch today to trick her into thinking that I am okay. Tonight on *Boy Meets World*, Topanga told Cory that she is still in love him. They actually k-i-s-s-e-d on the jungle gym at the end, and maybe they will get back together again. I wish my jungle gym story was as good as that one. All I can say is that Gina definitely doesn't wear our old friendship bracelet anymore.

Sincerely,
Ellie Beck

PS, I'm sorry to ask, but what does the word *gay* mean? It's a bad word, right? Actually, never mind, don't answer that. I think I already know.

Sunday, April 19, 1998

Hello,

Sorry I haven't written in a while. I can't say why. I could sleep for a thousand years, but I can't sleep. Life feels so different now and I feel like I've seen the world change ten times over, just like Dad says. Don't worry, I didn't get my "thing at the end of a sentence." I just need to talk to somebody, somebody real. I tried talking out loud a little bit today, but I don't like a thing that I said. I really hope that God can read and not just listen.

Luckily we got to skip Ruth's grave at the abandoned mine without Dad in the car today. I kept my knees tucked into my seat belt and held my hairy legs all the way to the doctor. It was so blue outside. I played the no talking game and counted birds, five points for each one sitting on the electric poles, ten points for each one flying, and automatically one hundred points if a bunch of them make that V-shape in the sky. I would automatically lose all of my points if a deer crossed the road.

Riding in the car with Mom makes the no talking game way too easy, though. She handed me another animal-themed coloring book, and I wished I could tell her that I would much rather draw. I wish I could tell her that I actually like what I did to my own hair. I wish I could tell her about all about the places I go to when I stare into space when I'm at the breakfast table and Dad is still sleeping in my room. Mom is too busy pretending we live in the imaginary world that she made for herself. She likes to say over and over when she's behind the wheel: "You'll thank me for this one day." She always says that just when things feel at their very worst.

The Sunday doctor told me "You will know what you really want when you are older." She thinks it's normal for kids to not know what they want to be when they grow up, and maybe one day I will know my true direction. Then she reminded me for the eighth week in a row, "In the meantime, you should really consider making new friends. Don't you want that for yourself, Ellie?" I really hate it when she says that.

It's actually impossible to play the no talking game with her because it's only two of us in such a small room with hardly any art in it. She has fake curly hair and shoulder pads to make her body a different shape. She keeps the pen above her right ear until she thinks something interesting happens. She always swallows a little bit before she writes things down and gives me advice, like she knows she is telling a lie too.

When we're together, I use a voice so small that I can barely hear myself. I don't even want to hear what I say in there. I honestly can't even tell any of it to you because I don't want you to accidentally think it's what I'm really praying for. I wouldn't ever tell her what's really bothering me, like the smell of my dad's breath. She already thinks that I am crazy. I felt so bad after today's session that I thought about writing an "I'm sorry" letter to myself, to Sofie and her family, and to pretty much everything I love. I wonder what that lady would think of me if we had met somewhere else, like at Freedom Valu's or at a baseball game. Would she still think that I'm sick? Would she want to be one of the new friends that I'm supposed to find? I don't want new friends. I put a rock on Sofie's porch nearly every day for a reason.

On the way back home, I fixed my headband and kept my coloring book shut tight on my lap. I didn't want to think about colors. I didn't want to think about anything at all. I watched Mom through the rear-view mirror. She kept her eyes on the road while we listened to the oldies station. Her green eyes had bags under them, heavier than usual. I wonder how they got there, because I always thought she was a heavy sleeper. I don't know, sometimes I feel like I have bags too even when nobody else can see them. I decided to close my eyes just enough to make it look like I was sleeping. It didn't last long.

Mom turned down "Build Me Up Buttercup" to tell me the "I am so proud of you" speech all over again. She just went on and on about it too. She didn't care if I was pretend-sleeping. Maybe this is bad to say, but I'm starting to care less about whether or not anybody is proud of me.

Once we got to a streetlight, she took a break from talking to dig through her purse. She seemed excited to tell me another long story, but first she put on her purple-red lipstick to maybe make it sound better. She then blabbed about how I'm now looking cute enough to come back to church with her and Dad. She even said, "I was just on the phone with Gina's mom, and we were thinking of signing you girls up for next year's Bible Study Youth Group. Wouldn't that be nice?"

Mom looked back at me in the rear-view mirror. She rubbed her lips together to spread the color, and waited for me to be grateful.

I have to admit, there are some parts of church I miss. The music is good, the bathrooms are always clean and empty. I especially miss the church potlucks when Dad's old work friend brings venison soup, those good frozen biscuits, and even beef-filled pasties with rutabaggies. It docsn't mean I would get to stop going to the doctor, though. That work friend might not even be at church anyways because he had to go to the doctor too. I heard that he hurt himself trying to drink and snowmobile at the same time. I wonder what he gave up for Lent.

The streetlight turned green and then Mom reminded me for the second time today, "Your hair is growing back so cute now." In case you didn't know, my hair is past my ears at this point. I feel like it's always in the way. I wish I could have given it all up for Lent. Mom said some other stuff too as we went down the hill, like how I should get highlights in my hair before middle school starts. I don't know why she would want me to highlight my least favorite part about myself, but then she said, "Your dad and I both think that would be so pretty on you." That's when I stopped listening and went back to looking at the sky.

Do you ever think "I want to go home" on your way home, but you're thinking of wanting to go somewhere else completely? Just once I would love a compliment from my family that's actually for me. Here are some for you: I like that you spend enough time looking at the sky to find this balloon. I like that you might keep my letter even when I'm too afraid to ever look at it again. I like that you're here even when I feel alone. There's probably more compliments I could tell you, but I just don't know them yet.

Sincerely,
Ellie

PS, I'm sending you this on Monday, April 20, all the way from Portage Lake. Just between us, I lost one of my bottom baby teeth after writing my letter last night. I didn't want to leave it under my pillow because I didn't want to give anyone a reason to come in my room to look there. I started to think that maybe I really was sick. I crawled out of my bed and pulled out my old Fisher-Price medical kit from when I was a little kid. I found the yellow plastic stethoscope tangled in the bottom of the bag and tried listening to my own heart. I could hardly hear anything. Dad came to my room anyways.

Maybe he was proud of me for doing good at the doctor, but I think he would have kissed me good-night no matter what I said about myself. Luckily, he didn't take my baby tooth or any other part of me. Please don't tell anyone, but I actually put the tooth in the trash just to be safe. I hope it at least ends up in the same pile as my old milk carton.

Rowan

Hello,

The Sunday doctor is happy I'm back at church again, but I'm not sure if anyone watching me there really loves me or means it when they say "Peace be with you." On my first day back at Mass, I saw dad's old work friend in a wheelchair from his snowmobile accident. I bet he still goes to the doctor too. He didn't bring anything to the potluck, but Mom says I came back on a good day. The priest talked a lot about "lawlessness" in a serious voice. He told a story about a guy in the Bible named David saying he's sorry, but he still needed to know the consequences for not being a good son to his father. I wonder if Mom thinks of me as her son now, but probably no such luck.

Anyways, I'm mostly writing to let you know that Sofie has been back in school because she has her nice aunt visiting from Detroit to help out. I'm really glad about it. I found Sofie wearing a cool peasant shirt with big sleeves by the flagpole, and I did a little dance in my head. Since she has been away, Sofie's hands have gotten new calluses and her baby sister has been learning more words, *Hi, Mama,* and even *Papa.*

Sofie and I have been having our bathroom stall meetings every day too. Our confident walks are really coming along with less and less time looking at the floor. Right before our practice today, we had a big conversation between our stalls. She told me, "Papa wrote me back yesterday." I could feel her smile through the cold metal walls. Richard told her that he now has a special job where he makes like ten cents an hour, like people did back a hundred years ago. Honestly, that's barely enough to buy a balloon a day. I don't know, he must feel awfully alone. How long do you think a person can possibly be alone for anyways? I can hardly do it for a weekend.

Sofie then said, "I'm going to learn a new song for him too, and I will sing it for him when he comes home one day." I just listened and kept my cheek against the wall listening to her to say more about her dad and how much he loves music. When we finally got out of the stalls, Sofie and I made really nice eye contact. It has felt like forever since we did that. I promised later that day to keep watch for her when she secretly used the school computers to check the brand-new website that the sheriff's department made. She wanted to see if she could help Richard come home sooner than later, but I guess the website didn't say much about that.

For now, I have plans to mail Richard a letter with all the words to a really good movie. That way, he can read it over and over again without needing a TV. I know he loves hero movies, so I'm debating between *Hercules* and *Matilda*. If you can, maybe you can send him a nice postcard or something too. His name is Richard Gavia, and he is at Marquette Hickory Prison. Even if things with my dad aren't great, I hope he never ends up there. I hope it's okay I said that. I just don't think prison is a good place for anybody.

Rowan Beck

PS, Sorry, one more thing real quick. I didn't tell anybody why, but at indoor recess I finally asked Sofie if she and Viivi have seen that Teletubbies show. All she knew was there is a character that's just a laughing baby that lives in the sun. To think that Gina called *me* weird. I tried to keep my conversation with Sofie quiet, though, because Nathan Lucas kept looking over at us. I kind of think he's a new spy for the Lambda Kappa Kappa Trampoline Club. My old friends all looked busy playing Animorphs and turning from humans to alligators and cheetahs, so it was hard to tell.

Anyways, good night. Bye.

Hi,

This letter has four balloons attached to it and you're probably wondering why. Well, I have a secret to tell you. I cut my hair a little bit after school today. Nobody but you can find out because I don't want to get locked out again. I think it's small enough so most people won't notice anyways, but at least I can feel the difference. I did it fast in the bathroom using my craft scissors. This time, I made sure to clean it all up really super good and picked up every little strand off the tile. I wasn't so sure where to hide the pieces, so I decided to put them all in this little sandwich bag. Luckily, I have been saving some of my quarters from the weeks I didn't write, and got four balloons strong enough to fly the bag away. Haven't you ever taken a big risk for something that seemed so small?

Well, there's actually a reason I cut my hair today. It's another big secret, and you really have to promise not to tell anyone. Like, a cross your heart, hope to die, stick a needle in your eye kind of promise.

Mom and I went to Freedom Valu's yesterday for her usual Mitch and Mary radio bingo cards. I chilled in the candy aisle because it's not like I'm old enough to gamble anyways. They didn't have my favorite Spice Girls gum, but they did have my second-favorite kind with a rainbow zebra on the wrapper. As I reached toward it, I noticed there was a lady or a man right next to me. I don't know what this person would call his or herself, but he or she had short hair. It was like really short hair, spiky and brown, and he or she also had long eyelashes. This person smelled like the hardware store and was only a few inches taller than me. Most of all, their nose had a ring in it, and they carried a big container of orange juice by their side.

I felt them looking over my shoulder and I started to sweat a little. They said "Excuse me" in a deep, raspy voice. I almost forgot to move. They were just inches away and grabbed a granola bar that said something about eating breakfast all day on the wrapper. This person looked healthy and like they were surviving just fine. I bet they even had their own house and car, and they are growing up to be the best they can be. His or her haircut was really nice too. Did I already tell you that? I don't know. I watched them push their hand through their spikes, and I said to them all in one breath, "I like your hair." He or she smiled in such a nice way, it was like we knew each other.

Before I had the chance to say anything else, he or she unzipped their leather jacket and walked away. They got in line next to my mom and the beef jerky. I hope that Mom saw the stranger and had a good thought about them too. I could still see their nose piercing shine even under the crummy lights from across the room. But when it was time to go, Mom called the name Ellie from all the way across the store. She said it three times, each time louder than the next. I put down the pack of rainbow gum and brushed hard. It was horrible. That person with the nose ring looked over at me with squinty eyes. I bet they knew that I'm not really an Ellie. I don't know why I think that, I just do. Gosh, it felt like they were my guardian angel or something. A guardian angel who drinks orange juice. Lookit, here's a drawing of the two of us together under a lighthouse. That's me on the left with the kind of hair I really want.

me and my orange juice angel!

I wish I really knew this person. I wish I thought to ask for their name to somehow include them in a game of MASH and find out where I'm going to live, what I'm going to eat, and who I'm going to marry. It would be so cool if their name was Rowan too. Or what if they had a name that I've never heard before in my entire life? I might never find out until I'm old enough to have a car and get gas and orange juice at Freedom Valu's all by myself. I'm now more determined than ever to get there.

I actually loved riding home with my mom after all that because I knew I didn't just make the whole thing up. She for sure saw what I saw, and maybe Mom will tell the doctor she realized that I don't have to grow up to look like her. Either way, Mom turned up the happy "Come On Over" song on her Shania Twain tape, and I realized it really is springtime. I think Shania would look really nice with a ring through her nose too.

I tried to describe the gas station guardian angel person to Sofie at our bathroom meeting today, but she didn't know them either. She scratched her head trying to think about any adults she knew with their nose pierced like that. Is it weird to think about someone you don't know this much? I don't know, because after that Sofie told me she has been thinking a lot about Howie from the Backstreet Boys. I didn't even know what to say after that. To be honest, it made me feel a little weird to hear her talk about boys. We hardly ever talk about that kind of stuff. Can you choose who you love?

Sorry. Anyways, I hope you like all of the balloons I sent this time. You can do whatever you want with the bag of hair. Maybe just throw it away. In the meantime, if you know who the gas station person is, maybe leave me their name or yellow book page under the WELCOME TO HOUGHTON: BIRTHPLACE OF NATIONAL HOCKEY sign. You know, the one next to Portage Bridge? In the meantime, here's another drawing. It's going to take me a while to shade it in right, but it's me a lot of years from now looking happy.

Thank you.

Love,
Rowan Beck

Hey-lo,

Guess what. I have been doing my best confident walks yet.
I can now keep my eyes off the floor when I walk out of the
bathroom stall, even when my leg hair peeks out of my capri
pants. Sofie and I even joked about writing in the bathroom
stall "EXPAND!" just like the chalkboard in Mr. B's class. I
just always try to remember how confident-looking that
nose-piercing person was last week at Freedom Valu's. I'll
never forget how they even had their orange juice at their hip
and free hand in their hair. His or her elbows were pointed
like wings. I wonder if that person has a lot of secrets too.
I wonder what they believe in. I've been noticing that the
fewer secrets I keep, the more confident my walk really feels.

I wasn't going to tell you this, but something else really
big happened the other day. I decided to tell Sofie one of my

233

biggest secrets, so please be careful with this letter after you read it. When we got out of school, Sofie and I watched the Trampoline Lambda Kappa Kappa Club climb into a carpool with that "I just want to fly" song playing real loud. I even saw Nathan Lucas's dad pull up his truck behind them with a wave and a fresh shave. I should have felt more alone then, but I felt okay standing right where I was. I tapped on Sofie's shoulder and said, "Let's walk."

When we got far enough down the hill, I told her, "My dad comes in my room some nights." I felt a big lump in my throat, and I suddenly didn't know enough to say more. She looked down, thinking. I almost regretted what I said because I don't want her to think that Dad is what makes me a messed-up girl when I'm actually a messed-up boy.

I held my own hands and asked the sky, "I'm still like a boy, right? Boys can still get hurt, right?" Sofie finally looked up and did a small nod. In that moment, I remembered her dad. She said, "Yeah, boys can still get hurt." It was really nice to have her listen, but it was hard, maybe hard for both of us. It almost felt like I was talking about somebody else's life. Sofie reached over and squeezed my hand as if she was trying to keep me from floating away.

To be honest, I cried a lot when I got home that afternoon because I felt a part of me come alive. Like, I don't know, maybe things won't be like this forever? Do you know what I mean? Maybe you don't know. Sorry.

You don't have to burn this letter or anything like that, but please don't tell anybody what I said. I'm still figuring things out, but for now I guess it's less of a secret than it was before.

Rowan

Hi,

Since the last time I wrote, things at my house are pretty much the same. The only difference is that Mom and Dad have been a little bit louder and I care less when my dad talks about "doing his best." After listening to them last night, I realized he's not doing his best at all. It's making me think more about the gas station guardian angel person and even Sofie's dad, and how different they are from my dad. Maybe there are a lot more ways to be a boy than I thought. I don't know. I don't really want to talk about all that right now. You know why? It's because I learned that not all secrets have bad feelings. Some secrets have good feelings, even if it's in a confusing way.

I will say that Sofie hasn't shared any of her biggest secrets with me. I know that she doesn't have to, but the school year is nearly over and the mosquitos are starting to come out. I decided to try asking her about it today in the girls' room. At the end of lunch, I waited inside of my favorite stall for her famous see-through sandals to show up under the door. Of course the Trampoline Club and all their new members showed up with their purple-and-white shoes instead. I tucked my legs into the door to make life easier for all of us.

Only one of the girls actually had to use the toilet, and the rest of them just stood at the three sinks blabbing about their weekend plans to go to the same skating session as some "cute boys" from class. They must have said "cute" a million zillion times, the very word the Trampoline Club gave me so much trouble for. I swear, crushes and the "the part" in *Titanic* are all anybody seems to be talking about anymore at recess, at lunch, and even before school. And get this—Courtney said she's going to try holding Dylan Beaman's hand during the slow skate on Saturday. This would be a major deal because three out of five girls talking today seem to like-like him too. I learned in math class that would be sixty percent of the girls, which is kind of a lot. The truth is, I put the valentine I made for Dylan Beaman in the trash weeks ago. It was much harder than it sounds because there's still a part of me waiting for him to change his mind about me. Courtney has a much better chance with him, though. She has a girl name and glitter on her lips.

After Courtney shared her big skate rink plan, everybody giggled some more about Dylan Beaman and some guy I've never met named Jack Dawson. I don't know. That's when the only bathroom-goer finally finished peeing, and they all started singing that "near, far, wherever you are" *Titanic* song in emotional voices. I don't know why they always walk around doing that. Needless to say, I enjoyed the peace and quiet once they left for the hallway. I took a deep breath and stretched out my legs until they cracked. But when I finally saw Sofie's feet, I got a big burst of energy like a Pixy Stix sugar rush.

I swung the stall door open. It banged against the tile wall so loud that I bet the boys' room could hear it. Sofie stood there holding the Rubik's Cube that her nice aunt gave her. Sofie said, "Sometimes you have to make it messy until you find the answer." She's so smart. She has already solved that thing like four times this week, and still finds it fun and interesting. Maybe she'll end up in the Guinness Book of World Records one day.

Instead of asking about one of her biggest secrets like I had planned, I surprised myself. I blurted out really fast, "Have you ever had a crush before?" I don't know why I felt so nervous right after asking her that. Everyone and even *Tiger Beat* magazine talk about it like it's no big deal. I almost wanted to take my crush question back, like maybe I should have saved it for the dark basement or at least for when we're in different stalls.

My toes curled up as I prepared myself to hear her say, "Duh, I have a crush on the Backstreet Boy Howie."

But then Sofie stopped playing with her Rubik's Cube  and smiled a new smile, just when I thought I have seen all of her smiles. This one changed the color of her cheeks and made her eyes the shape of crescent moons. I'll draw a picture of it for you so you can see it. I'll add some stars in the background too, just because that seems like the right thing to do.

Based off of this picture, can you tell if she was smiling at me? Or do you think she was smiling at someone in her head? I kind of hoped that she was smiling at me. I also hope that there is room for me in her head too. It's hard to know where I want to fit when all I want is to be a lot of things to her. I don't know.

Before Sofie could even open her mouth, three skinny girls with big earrings walked into our fifth-grade girl's room. One of them even had two piercings on the same ear.

They were actually the high schoolers who come to read to the little kids at William Henderson Elementary. They just ignored us to gossip and fix their eyes in the three mirrors. One of them even looked behind at our bathroom stalls to say, "Oh my God, everything in here is like tiny enough for babies." Sofie and I looked at each other and made our way toward the door. We both held on tight to our lunch boxes as we walked through the crowded hallway without saying a word. I just hope that Sofie doesn't think of our bathroom stalls as too small after we graduate from here.

She never did answer my question about crushes, but there must be somebody she likes other than Howie the Backstreet Boy. Either way, I put a Backstreet Boys poster in my room so she could see him if she ever comes over again. I guess it's okay not to know what Sofie thinks about, right? I'm trying my best to listen and not always try to figure out everybody's thoughts like a puzzle.

Anyways, if you want to, you can share a secret too. Maybe you can write it down somewhere or tell a friend? It doesn't really matter what kind of a secret it is, it's just good to try sharing sometimes.

Love you,
Rowan

Hi.

I went to Sofie's house today. We didn't ask any more about secrets or play more truth or truth, and I'm glad we took a break from that. It was just a nice, regular visit on a rainy day. Her visiting aunt showed us really old pictures of Sofie's parents and made us lemonade from a can.

After that, Sofie and I took Gushers up to her room to listen to her Selena tape. When we got to the song "Dreaming of You," Sofie closed her eyes and laid down on her old roadmap rug. I ate my snack while she mouthed the words. I'm hoping to learn some of those lyrics before I have my long drive to the doctor lady tomorrow. I think it will help.

I really hope that you get to listen to Selena sometime too. She's actually an angel now, but Sofie says that she still says hi to her poster every morning. Sofie also wants to get a nice farm tractor someday because Selena never lived long enough to get the one she wanted. My favorite Selena song is the first one on the tape. It's called "I Could Fall in Love." I actually haven't told anybody that before. I just don't want people asking questions and finding out who I'm thinking about when it's playing. That's what the song is kind of about anyways.

Hope your day has been good too.

Your friend,
Rowan Beck

Thursday, May 21, 1998

Hi,

For the past few nights, Mom has been sleeping on the couch under the DANCE LIKE NOBODY IS WATCHING sign. She looks awfully tired. I know this isn't true, but maybe it's because she has been up dancing all night. This morning I actually sat next to her until she woke up. There was something nice about seeing the morning sun on her face. Anyways, she wants me to do some extra chores so she can get a nap in before Dad comes home from work. He's almost always gone way past the T-shirt store hours, so who knows how late that will be. Mom told me that if I do really good cleaning up that she will bring home extra suckers and maybe a free pen from her bank job. She's trying to make everybody happy, but I'm not sure if it's going to work.

But before I go help out, I have something very important to tell you. It's really bad news. Sofie and Viivi have to go
to their grandparents' house for the summer because Mrs.
Gavia has to work so much and Richard is still gone. I guess
they're lucky to have grandparents, because all of mine
have passed away, but their grandparents live all the way in
Detroit. That's all the way in the bottom of the Mitten and so
many hours away. I guess Sofie seems a little happy about it
because Detroit has places we only see commercials for, like
Chuck E. Cheese and whatever. However, I don't think Sofie
realizes that my allowance won't cover a calling card for
long-distance phone calls. What if her grandparents don't
even have a phone?

Sofie said that she already tried begging her mom to let
her stay home in Houghton, but no such luck. She practically shouted, "It doesn't make sense that I have to be farther
from Papa than ever." She and Viivi have to drive down with
her aunt just a day or two after school gets out, and she'll be
gone for almost all of summer vacation.

It's not like I have the money to take a plane to see her
either. Gosh, I wonder how many balloons it would take to
fly over Mighty Mac Bridge, and all the way to Detroit. Or
maybe I will need a flock of seagulls, like in *James and the Giant
Peach*? Maybe I could sail with our refrigerator box? Sorry,
I'm being super silly right now. I know. It's just that I'm going
to miss Sofie so much and maybe she's having a hard time

with it too. Why can't they just let Richard out of that stupid place in Marquette, so everything can go back to normal and be okay for Sofie?

I'm especially sad about missing her birthday coming up. We were supposed to go downtown to see *Mulan* together, wave at the cars at Bridge Fest, and then sit on the sample tractors at Copper Country Mall's until Sofie found the one she liked best. At the end the day, we talked about going to the restaurant in Kmart. I was really looking forward to all of that. It was going to be a perfect day, the perfect summer where I didn't have to be at home and maybe Richard would finally come home. I wish I knew what to do. I know that everybody says that summer here is gone in a blink of an eye, but last summer was so hard. I won't ever really understand what it's like to be Sofie, but I just wanted this summer to be better for all of us.

Darn it, I have to go now. My mom is calling me for chore time. I'll say more soon.


Rowan


PS, Hi again. Dusting the living room for Mom wasn't so bad at all because I got to start the *Boy Meets World* season finale. Luckily I thought ahead and taped it last Friday. A lot of big things have happened in the episode so far. The teacher, who is always somehow around, gave them their last ever high school assignment. Everyone had to write "what's in their hearts." That sounds like something Mr. B would do. It's too bad that Dad got home before I could finish the episode, though.

Usually I try to hide in my room or behind furniture when he first gets home, but there was no time. I turned off the TV trying to look innocent just doing chores as he took off his shoes. Dad didn't even look at me, though. He just asked "Where's Mom?" in a mad and sad way. I almost didn't want to tell him because she and I both know how he can get on the "warpath," as she calls it.

I don't know. My heart just says I need to have a friend this summer or maybe find that gas station guardian angel again.

Hope you're okay.

Sincerely,
Rowan

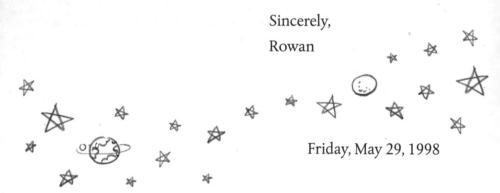

Friday, May 29, 1998

Dear Whoever You Are,

I'm probably the only person in the whole entire world who's going to miss being in school this summer. I just get a bellyache when I think about being stuck in the house these next few months. Even knowing I have just a few days left at William Henderson Elementary makes me feel a little weird. I'm mostly going to miss my favorite bathroom stall, the giant rock at recess, and having time to play. Meanwhile, everybody just seems excited because next year we're going to be at a huge school with electives, lockers, and its own swimming pool. Like always, I've been having trouble getting excited about the things I'm supposed to be excited about, especially today. Summer felt so close with warm air blowing through the classroom windows this afternoon.

I have to admit, I am glad I have summer vacation to take a break from science class. We're on pretty much the last unit now, learning about magnets. Even though magnets are really everywhere around us, in outer space and even under the ground, it seems like most of us didn't know much about them at all. Everyone had a lot of questions. I was super surprised when Nathan Lucas raised his hand for the very first time in the history of ever. He asked with a voice-crack at the end, "How can these little waves that we can't even see have so much power?" I thought it was a good question, but some kids giggled about it and called him a "sissy." I can see why he doesn't usually raise his hand. Are there things that also keep you from asking what you want to? I sure know there are for me.

Anyways, after that, one of the big paper football players said to the teacher, "I also don't really understand the whole opposites attract thing. Can't anything just stay where it is even if it's attracted to something else?" Mr. B thought about that one for a minute and then finally replied, "Nothing that's for us will pass us by." I guess that makes sense.

That whole time, Dylan Beaman was eating string cheese next to me, pulling it apart layer by layer until only the wrapper was left. He was wearing a cool Godzilla shirt. Dylan then cracked his back with a twist, and put the smelly wrapper onto my desk as if the leftovers were for me. I picked it up and crumpled it into a ball. That was actually the closest I got to getting a note passed to me all year long, which is kind of sad. My old friends used to pass me notes with smiley faces, tic-tac-toe challenges, and rumors about the Mona Lisa painting in the art room moving her eyes. Now they probably pass "yes, no, maybe" notes about crushes, who is going to get their period next, and things I'm not supposed to know about.

I thought those girls were going to get into big trouble today for passing notes and not paying attention, but it seemed like Mr. B didn't care at all. I was so surprised, everyone was surprised actually. Instead, Mr. B said, "If you have something to say, you can try sharing it with the whole room." Before everybody could say "awwwwww" together, Mr. B went behind his desk and pulled out a brown box full of this year's yearbooks. Then he said, "Why don't you write in each other's books instead of passing notes?" I don't know how he manages to make everything into a good lesson, even when we are technically doing bad things and following our own directions. He carried the box of yearbooks around the room and handed them out to us one by one.

Pretty much everyone cheered and scrambled to look at the pictures inside of each other's books, even though they are all exactly the same. I stared at the one in front of me before pulling it safely onto my lap. The yearbook was heavier than I expected. The front cover was shiny plastic, stamped with the words *Sweet Memories*. There was a collage on the first page I opened to. The black-and-white photos looked so old already, especially the ones from the very first day of the fifth grade. Somehow they got a picture of me with my headband and empty backpack standing next to the flagpole outside. I wish they asked me first before using that one. I look so silly in it smiling with no teeth showing and no friends to hug my shoulders.

Mr. B shouted over everybody's chatter, "This room was made for us to appreciate each other, so go ahead and share your yearbooks with your fellow classmates." I know he wanted us to help each other remember the good parts of ourselves and of our year, but it's just not that easy for me. I wasn't so sure who would even want to write in mine and I sure as heck didn't want to write the name Ellie in anybody else's. So instead I hid my yearbook inside my desk while everybody else was laughing, taking out their gel pens, and getting in line to talk to each other. I couldn't believe the yearbook was called *Sweet Memories*. I was really over the whole thing, but Mr. B made his way through the crowds.

He leaned over my desk and said, "Ellie, why don't you just leave your book open and see what happens?" I really didn't want to, but I listened to Mr. B anyways. At first, nobody walked up to my yearbook and I went to the pencil sharpener for a few minutes just so people didn't think I actually cared. I kept my nose to the wall and pressed in my pencil so hard that it broke. Re-sharpening it gave me an excuse to stay there a little longer and let the room disappear.

You won't believe it, though. When I got back to my seat, the Trampoline Club walked over. Well, they were technically lining up to sign Dylan's book at the desk next to mine. Even so, they stood in front of me and each wrote their names into my book using their most boring-colored pens. I was so surprised that I forgot to say hi. My old friends could have used their glittery gel pens or added a simple HAGS, which is a cool new way of saying "Have a great summer."

When they moved on to Dylan's yearbook, I read and reread their names, Courtney, Mary, and Gina, over and over again. I'm still not so sure what I want to remember from this year at all. Practically everyone stood in line to write something for Dylan. Some people gave him their home phone numbers. Even Nathan Lucas wrote his. I wouldn't think he even knows how to talk on the phone. I admit, I didn't bother writing anything at all in Dylan's book. I bet he didn't notice, because he didn't write in mine either. It's whatever, though.

I used to daydream that I could rewind time all the way back to a year ago. I never would have asked to play Uncle Jesse in our *Full House* game. I would have never gone to that slumber party where I said that thing that made everyone feel weird. I would have never folded away my shirt with an **E** written in rhinestones or danced under that streetlight. I used to imagine all my old friends doing cool jumps off the trampoline and landing in a nice circle around me. After that, Dylan Beaman would buy me a lifetime supply of potato chips that have vinegar and sea salt. I can promise you that's not my dream anymore.

I really wanted to play Uncle Jesse and I meant what I said at that slumber party, so I don't need their fake nice yearbook signatures anyways. Haven't your dreams ever changed? You might be surprised to hear this, but Sofie and I didn't even write in each other's yearbooks. Maybe it was still too scary to do that in front of everyone in class, but I like what we did instead.

At recess, we sat in the dewy grass under the secrets tree. We cut out each other's Picture Day pictures on page thirty-two with enough room to punch out little holes at the top. I used purple yarn and she used green yarn, and we each laced our photos into real friendship necklaces and tied our own knots. At the end, we wasted no time in putting them around each other's necks.

Our pictures flapped around in the breeze better than capes. The yarn twirled and tickled the back of my neck, but that wasn't the only reason I was smiling. Sofie can now still be there even when it seems like I'm all alone at my bedroom window or on my long drives this summer. I know I probably won't be using my confident walk and will look down at the ground a lot. At least now I know that I can look down, and see a picture of my friend making her "Are you kidding me?" face. When I noticed my own Picture Day picture around Sofie's neck, I decided that it doesn't matter if it shows my fake smile and wrong hair. What matters is that Sofie wears it knowing that there are other parts of me.

She even said, "I like these necklaces so much that I might write a song about them. Maybe we could make extras to hang as ornaments on next year's Christmas trees too." I tried not to look too excited about that, but it really did make my heart big. I held on to her picture around my neck so tight that it folded into my hands, and nobody could tattle-tell on us for being too close.

All of my friendship necklaces with old friends had come from the store. The silver usually scratched off, or one of us would lose our half of the friendship pact. Or sometimes other groups of friends had the exact same friendship necklaces, even if their friendship was nothing at all like ours. I didn't realize until today that I have never had homemade friendship necklaces with someone before. Wearing each other right over our hearts means that we won't ever pass each other by. I think Sofie is going to mail a picture of herself to Richard too. I think it's a great idea.

Even though my mom's birthday isn't until August, my dad got her a brand-new necklace too. It actually reminds me of that blue necklace the bad guy had on the *Titanic*, but way less fancy. I bet Mom will wear it to church on Sunday and tell everyone how good he is at being a husband. Meanwhile, all the husbands will just talk about the weather or whether or not the Red Wings will win the Stanley Cup again. Did you know that's what people talk about at church when they're not talking about God? Anyways, Dad is just trying to keep their marriage okay and show that he loves Mom or whatever. I'm trying really hard to love him, but it's not always easy.

Him being extra nice again makes me feel like I just made everything up. Maybe I told Sofie the wrong secret about him coming into my room. I don't know. He has been really good lately and put all of his glass bottles on the high shelf, even with these big hockey games on TV to celebrate. Necklaces are powerful, I guess. I can't stop looking at the one around my neck, though I will probably hide it underneath my T-shirt on Sunday so nobody asks me any questions.

Thanks for listening, and don't forget to put on bug spray.

Rowan Beck

Thursday, June 4, 1998

Dear You,

Today was the very last day of elementary school. I'm trying my best to look on the bright side of things. For example, I didn't even have to buy myself a balloon today. Mr. B gave one to each of us as a goodbye present. I will miss him, even though I didn't tell him that. I kind of wish I had. I don't know, it's weird to think of myself as a middle schooler now.

For these last few days at William Henderson, the classroom was so humid that I could practically swim in it. The hallways smelled like lemon cleaning supplies, and the trash filled up with everyone's worn-out folders. We all had to give back our language arts binders for the new fifth graders to use next year, and all of the inspiration posters were taken down. Every day, we watched the clock like it was the best teacher in the whole wide world.

For most people in my class, their favorite thing from this last week was probably the fifth-grade water balloon fight and eating Popsicles outside for Field Day. A lot of people also love that game where we fill a bucket with water by squeezing a wet sponge, and everybody screams. Not me, though. Today was the best because Sofie and I got to show everybody what we have been working on all along.

Just like the first day of school, Mr. B had us line up next to the big sunny window in the back of the room. This time, though, he wanted to try things a little bit differently, so he played dance music on his boom box for us to do our confident walks. The words in the first song he played said, "Welcome to your life, there's no turning back." I tapped my foot to the notes like I was born knowing them.

Dylan went first and did his walk the exact same as always, slow and steady in his Red Wings jersey. I bet a lot of people wrote "Don't change" into his yearbook. He stood tall and his shoes still lit up. He has probably been doing his walk like that since the beginning of time. Sofie, on the other hand, stepped bigger and louder than she ever did at school. Her walk was so confident that she didn't even care what music was playing. She mouthed the words to her "Shake, Shake, Shake" song, and rattled the brand-new gold beads in her hair into a musical instrument. The flying gold picked up the light from the window. She looked so much like Richard in that moment, glowing like she was already out in the sun.

At the end of her walk, Sofie blew a kiss to the whole room. I couldn't believe it. I had never seen her do that before. Do you think the kiss was really for everyone or do you think it was for someone special? Either way, she did a really great job.

When it was finally my turn, Mr. B said, "Rowan, you're up." It was like his words echoed through the whole entire room. He had never said my real name out loud before. Now that I think about it, I actually think that was my favorite part of the day. It made it much easier to "EXPAND!" just like the chalkboard said.

I took my first step and forgot the music was playing at all. I only heard the fan in the corner of the room. My cheeks blushed pink. I put my hands on my hips, and pretended that I had a leather jacket and a nose piercing. My friendship necklace swung with every step. I felt the whole room's eyes on my walk like they were meeting me for the first time. Mr. B reminded me I deserved to be there by calling me who I am.

When I got back in line with everyone else, I pulled my hand through my hair and took a big breath. If the teacher asked me again, I could probably think of ten things I love. One day, I might even be brave enough to write them in a bathroom stall with my permanent marker.

After everybody got their turn, Mr. B led the entire class past the recycling bin, and into the hallway to say goodbye to William Henderson Elementary School. We did our walks all together like a parade. All the little kids in the school smiled and gave us high fives from the sidelines like in the movies. I hardly remember the rest, it happened so fast. But I remember smiling and clapping with everybody else in my class just for making it this far.

I do hope that my confident walk stays with me when I start at a new school in September. Do you think it could leave and never come back? Sorry. I'm trying my best not to think like that, but sometimes I can't help it. It's just that tomorrow is my last chance to see Sofie in a long time. Odds are I'll have to run into the Trampoline Lambda Kappa Club over summer vacation, probably with our moms at Kmart or the strawberry festival or something like that. Our moms might even want to talk to each other, and my old friends and I would have to just stand there praying for it to be over. Then, on the ride home, I would have to find a way to tell my mom who I have really been having slumber parties with this spring. Gosh, I would be grounded for life if that happened.

To top it all off, the Spice Girls actually broke up. Sofie told me all about it just as we were leaving our elementary school for the very last time. The Spice Girls nearly split in their movie because of a mean spy, but I didn't think it would actually happen in real life. Do you think that anything good could happen next? Has their song "Viva Forever" ever made you cry? What about their song about moms? Either way, their songs are still the best for drowning out my parents' shouting downstairs, which is what I did this afternoon. Mom sounded extra upset, sad even.

I could hear the clanking of Dad taking his bottles down. I think I heard him punch his wall again too, but it's hard to tell. You would think he would be at least a little bit happy that the

Red Wings will probably win the Stanley Cup again. I don't know, though. Even with my loud music, I could hear him say "The world keeps turning around." I think he's mad or sad about something too. Maybe he just cares too much. Either way, now I know for sure that I didn't tell Sofie the wrong secret. I just wish I could remember more. I wish I could have a camcorder at the right time. In the meanwhile, here is a drawing of me and my mom driving somewhere that's not here.

Hope you're okay.

Sincerely,
Rowan


PS, I was just looking through my yearbook, and it's not as empty as I thought. I can't believe it. Mr. B actually left me a note in the back. It says, "Dear Rowan, Thank you for including me in your journey this year. Even in silence, your voice is so strong. You have a great gift for this world, and I know that can be a big, scary responsibility. If you ever need to talk to someone, you can always call 1-866-488-7386 or come visit me in my classroom next year. In middle school and beyond, keep on changing, keep doing the work, and keep your head up. With love, Mr. B."

I didn't know I could be thanked for any of that, especially when I have been feeling so bad this year. Maybe I'm not as bad as I thought? I don't know. Either way, maybe I have my own emergency contact now, someone to call when I feel lonely or confused. That's good news, I think.

Well, thanks for listening.


Love,
Rowan

Dear You,

Today was my last day with Sofie before she goes to Detroit. She told me that her grandparents live near a tire swing that her mom went to when she was a kid. I think that's great she gets to have that tradition. I think she's lucky to go, but I bet she will miss the rivers and trees and hills here. They're not the same anywhere else. I bet she'll miss a lot, especially her mom. I don't know. I guess I'll never know what it's like to be Sofie, but that's okay.

Sorry, it's just that I'm not so sure how to start this letter because I'm kind of afraid to tell you something.

Today was one of the best days of my life. I just thought it was going to be weird and sad because Sofie and I only had two or three hours left together, but I was wrong. What if we have our whole lives together?

Sofie and I galloped across the Portage Bridge from Houghton to Hancock with three yellow balloons. We sang that same song Hercules sings, "I will find my way, I can go the distance." We sang it louder than that last school bell ever could. Our balloons bounced through the air trying to catch up to us. Sofie took on the big part at the end of the song and shouted, "I will go most anywhere to find where I belong." She stretched her arms to the moon, faded into the blue sky like somebody had tried to erase it. We carried our balloons all the way to Mont Ripley.

We went past the pine trees, ski stunt equipment, and all the way to the bowl of the ski slope. In that moment, we didn't care about shouting "I'm king of the world" for the whole town to hear. Instead, we cared about each other, the white puffy clouds shaped like dolphins and other animals with good memories. I pointed up to the sky. It wasn't until today I told Sofie: "I like using balloons to send mail to far-away places that I don't always know how to get to." I tied one of our balloons to a nearby rock and said, "Let's use the other two to send something out for your dad." Sofie smiled and said "Yes" real big.

I pulled some markers out of my bag, and we got started right away. I'm not sure what Sofie's letter said, but she showed me a picture that she drew of her riding Richard's shoulders under a big bright light. She used shadow to make it look as 3D as possible. My letter to him included a really nice drawing of a Kit Kat bar split into two. Sofie and I carefully tied our letters to the ends of our balloons, and triple knotted the long ribbons just in case.

Sofie pointed into the distance and said, "When we let them go, let's each make a wish about anything we want." I thought it was a good idea, so I started our countdown of

"5, 4, 3, 2, 1, ZIGAZIG AHHH" to set the balloons free. We opened our hands and our letters chased after the sun, going up and up until they were farther than the welcome signs, water towers, and all the rivers in sight. It was almost hard to believe that they started in our very own hands.

We held our breath and quietly made our wishes. In my heart, I asked for something I have asked for before. I wished we would go somewhere that has five spare rooms and lemon trees in wintertime, and that we could stay there together with Richard and everyone all year round. Maybe I would bring my mom with me too so she's not stuck with Dad. I don't know. I just hope a place like that actually exists. I opened my eyes and played with my friendship necklace waiting for something to happen.

Sofie quietly let out her breath and put her hand up to her forehead to look for the sky mail one last time. She said to me, "It's good to tell each other our wishes because then maybe we can help each other make them come true." The last remaining balloons did a tiny little dance in the wind just hearing that. I told Sofie she could go first.

She blinked twice, and kissed my forehead. Her lips were even softer than her hands. That was her wish, her big secret, and there is nothing to forgive. I promise you, there is nothing to forgive.

I knew that things would never be the same again because the whole sky was watching and I had nowhere to look but up. Sofie reminds me that the moon is actually always there, even during the daytime. She rested the side of her head on mine, and her beads fell over my shoulder like a quilt. I felt safer than ever. I would usually ask for you not to tell anyone all of this, but I really don't think anyone would even believe it if you did. I've heard plenty of stories about girls and boys, but never one like this.

After all, Sofie Gavia is not a crush. She is a hand full of balloons, and I am going to miss her this summer because she has the maps to all of my favorite places. I hope you have things to look forward to too. I'm trying really hard right now, but I just want it to be today all over again.

Thank you,
Rowan Beck

Saturday, June 6, 1998

Dear Whoever Is Listening,

How are you? I'm lying on top of my bed and I'm feeling okay. I'm actually more than okay right now.

When I woke up this morning, though, I had a stomachache and I wondered for a moment if I had made a mistake letting Sofie kiss my forehead. I looked at the drawing of her orange couch I keep next to my bed. I touched it as if I were back there again. My parents went out for errands today, so I decided it was safe to call the number Mr. B put in my yearbook. I didn't know exactly who I was calling, but they seemed happy to hear from me and wanted to know all about my day before it even started. I didn't say much, but it still felt nice and they gave some good advice that I didn't even ask for.

After about five minutes on the phone, I said goodbye and tried not to cry. But I did cry. I don't think I shared anything wrong, but it's always easy to feel like I'm going to get into trouble for something. It's hard to know sometimes because my house, school, and some people who hardly know me want me to forget the important things. They want me to forget my name. They want me to forget who I love and they want to decide what I learn. They want me to think that God's hand has let go and doesn't care about me. Through my tears, I made a pinky-promise with myself to remember the important things tomorrow when we drive by the trees and abandoned mines on those long car rides to the doctor lady.

I wiped my eyes and tried to remember the one and only time I ever saw my dad cry. But I've seen my mom cry way more times. I put the home phone back in its normal spot in the hallway, and decided to take off my friendship necklace for the first time. I needed some time to think, and I took a long walk without Sofie by my side. I made it all the way to the big river by my house, and found a spot to sit near the army man statue and the Houghton welcome sign, where I used to check for letters. I watched the kayakers get carried down the stream, and I threw random rocks into the water knowing I would have no porch to put them on for the next few months. I thought about telling my mom about the phone call. I thought about everything that it could lead to if I told more people the truth about what it's like to be my dad's son. I think I will tell Mom, or at least try, because life didn't feel so scary anymore when I got back to my house a few hours later.

I stepped into my bedroom, and lost my breath. Nearly one hundred balloons completely covered my pink walls. There must have been at least ten different colors floating in every corner. I don't know how Sofie got inside the house, but I know that it was her because there was a piece of paper on top of my bed that said: "You gave me ninety-four rocks. Here are ninety-four balloons. When you have the chance, write me at my grandparents' house please. I'll check the mailbox every day. 20025 Greenfield Road, Detroit, MI 48235."

It made me so happy that I did a slow dance with the little paper. I can't wait to tell her thank you ninety-four times.

I cracked open my window, letting the wind move the balloons around me like a solar system. Their static hugged my hair, my fingers traced through the dancing ribbons. I can promise you now that I am going to sleep on top of my quilt tonight because the stars are right here. I can touch them. I can wish on them without even trying.

I know that balloons don't last forever. They might be on the ground or in a landfill tomorrow morning. I know my bedroom walls are still there and there will always be someone trying to keep them pink. I know that my mom might not believe me when I tell her about Dad. She might blame it on my boy haircut or call me crazy. You don't have to say anything to make me feel better about this stuff because I know that it's all true, and now I have that number to call again thanks to Mr. B.

And I have a kind of friend that I've never had before. We have the biggest ship in town, and in the fall we will take our box out of her basement. In the meantime, Sofie and I can remember each other when it feels easier to disappear. I'm going to write her a really nice letter tomorrow night, and maybe the night after that, and the night after that.

I don't really know what I'll be when I grow up, but I can say that I'm going to fill my house with rocks and balloons with Sofie Gavia. We will live with hills in Michigan, have a dog, drive a tractor. The wallpaper will be yellow like honey. We will have our own moon bounce and have framed maps to all of our favorite places hanging on the walls. There will be a long table, the fridge will be full, and we will have only one rule that says we cannot tell each other what is and isn't okay to eat. There will be valentines tied to the phones in case someone mean calls, and a whole entire yearbook filled with anyone nice to call. Oh, and there is another rule where we say yes to our feelings and "EXPAND!"

If I don't write balloon mail anymore, and spend my allowance on postage stamps instead, please remember one thing: My name is Rowan. I even told my dad today when he walked into my room tonight. He looked afraid of the magic, but I know that it will always be mine. He slammed the door and said, "You have a lot to think about."

He's right. I'm starting to smile when I think about what my life could be.


Love,
Rowan

# AFTERWORD

Monday, June 15, 1998

Hi Rowan,

I found your letter stuck in a tree not too far from my house in Calumet. I hope you don't mind that I read it. I actually found it a long time ago, back in March. I've been wanting to tell you since we were in class together, but I didn't know how to say it because it seems like you're quiet all the time too, kind of like you are hiding or something. I don't mean that in a mean way. I'm actually really glad I found your letter when I did. I have never gotten anything longer than a Christmas card before.

I mostly wanted to write and let you know that you're not left behind. I actually feel that way sometimes too. I haven't told anybody about this before, but sometimes I pray at night to fit in better. You asked if there's a place that helps me imagine again, and there is. I usually go there alone, though. It's my secret spot by the Pilgrim River, maybe not too far from where you stood in the sand. My spot doesn't have any sand, but has lots of moss that covers the big cedar trees. I sometimes pretend I'm there when I'm actually at the dinner table and I'm supposed to be following a bunch of rules. Grown-ups make so many rules.

I wasn't so sure how to start this letter, and now I'm not so sure how to end it. In your letter you said you didn't know if you could end it with the word *love*. Mom says there's all kinds of love, and when Dad's not around, I love everything. I'm still trying to figure out what it all means, but I can say that I love what I found in your letter. If you ask me, you're pretty lucky to have a good friend like you do. If you care that much about somebody, you have to hold on and not let go.

I taped four quarters onto the paper below. One is to buy another balloon and the last three you can save for the fall. We can share a chocolate milk when we get to middle school. I hope that's okay because I would really like a friend to sit next to.

Love,
Nathan Lucas

# AUTHOR'S NOTE

*The Ship We Built* is about many things. It is about beginnings: the realization that as a kid, so many ways of connecting and building exist. It is about that spark and strength that comes with realizations that are big and untaught. The book is also about big subjects, like coming out to yourself and others, surviving incest, having your world quietly change with the fall of different industries. Asking for help. Asking for things to end, begin. Living with wonder, and the joy and pain that comes with it.

This book is a gift to my ten-year-old self. I was nine when I stopped speaking at school. I was ten when I wrote my first suicide note. According to the American Academy of Pediatrics, more than 50 percent of teenage trans boys attempt suicide. This is the highest rate of any group under the LGBTQIA+ umbrella. Many trans boys, especially those with violent or absent fathers, struggle with not knowing what they can grow up to be. Many of us have been abused, and will never tell because many feel pressured to claim girlhood in order to be believed as survivors. When I came out as trans, I was told I was not trans. Instead, I was "a confused girl who had been abused." For a while, I regretted telling anyone anything at all.

Being trans increases the possibility of getting hurt by

strangers and loved ones and having fewer resources to deal with it. It raises questions of being lovable or being easy enough to understand. Being abused does not make you trans, and even if it did, it doesn't matter. What's important is you offer respect when someone shares a part of their identity or experience.

All this to say, I would not call this a "trans book" or an "abuse book." It's about the things I have had to carry shame about. It's a book about my hiding, Rowan's hiding. A book about the ache of constantly being out of place—to the point where you believe only the sky will understand. We have to question, as a society, what it means to protect somebody. What happens when we find emergencies in the wrong things? What happens when you love somebody who hurts you? And in Sofie's case, how does the absence of one person hurt an entire community?

Writing this has been one of the most deeply human experiences of my life. It is no small thing to explore the gap that existed between my reality and what I needed. It makes me sad and angry to know that it might not reach those who may need it the most. But I wrote this book because Rowans exist, and we need to see ourselves in books. Although this book is fiction, it also is not. There are also Sofies, Richards, and nameless moms and dads in your own community and tucked away in prisons. They are in the Midwest, and other places labeled as "backward," and often get left behind in conversations, actions, and resources.

Rowan's intimate letters are about the importance of having at least one person believe you and see you. Although he finds this in Sofie, Mr. B, and ultimately Nathan Lucas, I hope you could also be that person for Rowan. I also hope that somebody can be that for you. No matter what your experience is in reading this book, look up. Look for the balloon, look for what's left in the recycling bin. Look for who has an empty seat in class again and again. Look for everybody who is waiting to be seen.

# RESOURCES

**If you are a young person with a home like Rowan's,** know that it is not your fault. Someone hurting your body or feelings might feel normal for you, but it doesn't have to be. The change might be a scary one, some people might go away for a while or try to tell you that you're bad for wanting a better life. You are not bad. Everyone deserves a home to feel safe in and everyone deserves to sleep the whole night through. If there are no adults in your life you trust with your story, here are some numbers you can call:

> **Darkness of Light**, local information and resources on sexual abuse for children, teens, and adults.
> *1-866-367-5444*
> **National Child Abuse Hotline**, 24/7 crisis counseling in more than 170 languages and connection to thousands of emergency and support services.
> *1-800-422-4453*
> **National Runaway Safeline**, 24/7 crisis support and on and offline resources, and also offers a family reunification program.
> *1-800-786-2929*

**If you are a young person with questions about gender and**

love like Rowan's, know there is nothing wrong with you. You are growing and becoming. There are other kids and adults out there like you in this world even if you haven't met them yet. Some are thriving, some have even made their own families. Many are struggling and working hard to make a better world for you. In the meantime, your questions are perfect, and you are deserving of care no matter what. Here are some numbers you can call and websites you can visit:

**GLBT Near Me,** a directory of 15,000 support centers, youth groups, and community centers for gay, lesbian, bisexual, and transgender people of all ages.
*www.glbtnearme.org*

**LGBT National Help Center**, links and phone numbers to free peer-support and local resources.
*www.glbtnationalhelpcenter.org*

**Trans Lifeline,** a peer support line run for and by trans people. For hotline hours or information on micro-grants, visit www.translifeline.org.
*1-877-565-8860*

**The Trevor Project**, a 24/7 hotline for LGBTQIA+ people twenty-five years old and younger.
*1-866-488-7386*

**Trevor Space**, an international online community for LGBTQIA+ people thirteen to twenty-four years old.
*www.trevorspace.org*

**Upper Peninsula Rainbow Pride**, a non-profit organization for LGBTQIA+ community, events, and activities in the Upper Peninsula of Michigan.
*www.uprainbowpride.org*

**If you are a parent or mentor looking to lovingly support a child through navigating gender and sexuality**, first of all, know that change is not loss. Listen. Take a moment to realize there is no emergency, the focus should never be on the "cause" because nothing "went wrong." As with anything in parenting, you do not have to have all the answers. See the resources above or explore the websites below with your questions:

**Coming Out With Care**, an e-care package full of essays, a guided journal and coloring page, playlist, and more to support your journey with a young person who recently came out as anything under the LGBTQIA+ umbrella.
*www.mykidisgay.com/coming-out-with-care*
**Gender Spectrum**, offering resources for individuals, schools, and workplaces to make their spaces more gender inclusive.
*www.genderspectrum.org*
**Lighthouse**, a directory of LGBTQIA+ affirming therapists and healthcare providers for all ages.
*www.lighthouse.lgbt*

**PFLAG**, connecting parents of LGBTQIA+ people for events, advocacy, and support groups. In the Upper Peninsula of Michigan, there are two active chapters: PFLAG Keweenaw and PFLAG Marquette.
*www.pflag.org*

**Trans Youth Equality**, offering workshops, summer and fall camps, support groups, and other forms of advocacy for transgender children, youth, and families. They also partner with educators and service providers.
*www.transyouthequality.org*

**If you're an adult concerned with the safety of a child in your life and you don't know what to do,** educate yourself on the options immediately. In a vast majority of cases, children will not call a number for support the way that Rowan did. More likely, they will decide it's normal, deserved, or dissociate completely. Many will repeat it into their adulthoods, and may ormay not receive help then. For immediate guidance call the following number,

**STOP IT NOW!**
*1-888-773-2362*

# ACKNOWLEDGMENTS

In January 2014, Ilona, forever smart, loving, and dear, texted me, "You need to write a children's book." I sent her the first draft of *The Ship We Built* later that day.

In the making of this novel, bless those who helped me find the infinite ways to define a friendship, a relationship, a ship. Emily C and the Hungarian language for giving me a new relationship with the moon; Laura G for giving me a new relationship with everything. Andrea Gibson for teaching me the moon and streetlight are the same in "Birthday;" that icicles can heal wounds in "Maybe I Need You." Thank you to my first muse, *Altató* by József Attila, found on the street in Budapest. Paavo P, the first person to say "You are a boy, and I'm glad you met yourself." Adam A for saying "Nobody can do what you do." The Argentinian soccer team that gave me a toilet paper bouquet on a hard day; Lila L, Daniel L, David Tiselj's Shipwrecks-Co, Shelby Z, who have taught me a great deal about ships. Thank you Michael A for teaching me about endings. Thank you Nathan Michaelson, Brian Cari, Joe Karabatakis, Nick Bunker, Justin, Evan "Barty" Sachs, Jake Kosinski, and Yorrick Detreköy for offering what became the afterword and offering your understanding of a past few know.

Thank you, Susan Shapiro, Susan Rice, and Max the cat for helping me find this beginning. Charlotte Sheedy and Kelsey Klosterman, and the rest of the Charlotte Sheedy Literary Agency team for your incredible trust, the beautiful dimension and humanization you brought to a too often untold narrative. Madison B and Kelsey A, extraordinary librarians, and Futaba S, who at the earliest stages encouraged me to tell the truth even if it gets dark. Thank you Sean S and Linus I for reminding me that Rowan's story doesn't need clarity to have hope. Thank you a million times over to Nancy Mercado, Rosie Ahmed, and the team at Dial Books for Young Readers at Penguin Random House for asking all of the right questions. Thank you for reminding me that no matter where the balloon lands, there is always someone listening.

Thank you to those who gave this piece so much love and encouragement when it was only notebook pages, giving me permission to let it become something bigger. Namely, Sarah C, David Z, Kali C, Lena A, Rena B, Shoshana G, Zettie S, Tanya S, Maya S, Aaron K, Sawyer D, Lisa N, Alison K, Kevin D, Annie F, Chloe G, Daniel L, Alex V, Charlie P, Tom R, Amanda H, and Chris S. Angie Chen, who helped me piece the notebook pages together. Alison Bechdel, who now has all of those pages.

Gratitude to those who have lent their creative genius into creating many mediums of *The Ship We Built* leading to now. An animated short, thanks to Rosalie Eck and Harry Rubin-Falcone, that premiered at the Locomoción Festival de Animación in Mexico City. An art book of collages, mostly featuring artwork from the *Big Questions* series by Anders Nilsen, gifted to me by Sky S, and *Wings. Strings. Meridians.* by Tara Jane O'Neil. And eventually sweet Noah Grigni, who illustrated the insides and outsides of this very book in your hands. Thank you to THE STUDIO readers for the screenplay-in-progress, Paige, Rachel Burkhardt, Roseanne Almanzar, Lucas Van Engen, Adam Dulin Tavares, and Joslyn DeFreece, who was the first person to embody Rowan. Robert R, who has seen nearly every version of the story. Ally Sheedy, for your familial warmth, for continuing to write a million more drafts with me. You give me so much joy.

Gratitude for the songs that filled the text; namely, Selena Quintanilla's *Dreaming of You* album, and endless inspiration from the *Alas, Alas* album by Alas, Alas, "Favorite Tree" by Ilona Brand, and "Wrong-Righter" by Nicomo.

Gabrielle S, John T, Paul Aster S-T, and Cléa M, bless you for the dozens of kitchen table reads. Federico P for letting me read the entire freakin' thing out loud to you early on. Troy S, Victoria C, and Sofie the lamb for letting me read to you later on. Oliver M, Collin M, Llewie N, and Michael G for letting me read to you at the very, very end. Dana L and Rae M for being real (s)heroes at checking-in. Michelle F and